TWO
LINES

Two

THE
FUTURE
OF
TRANSLATION

World Writing in Translation
Issue 30, Spring 2019

**TWO LINES
PRESS**

EDITOR
CJ Evans

MANAGING EDITOR
Jessica Sevey

SENIOR EDITORS
Veronica Esposito
Michael Holtmann
Emily Wolahan

ONLINE EDITOR AND ASSISTANT EDITOR
Sarah Coolidge

FOUNDING EDITOR
Olivia Sears

DESIGN
LOKI

COVER DESIGN
Quemadura

SUBSCRIPTIONS
Two Lines is published twice annually.
Subscriptions are $15 per year;
individual issues are $12. To subscribe,
visit: www.twolinespress.com

BOOKSTORES
Two Lines is distributed by
Publisher's Group West.
To order, call: 1–866–400–5351

Two Lines
Issue 30
ISBN: 978–1–931883–87–0
ISSN: 1525–5204

© 2019 by Two Lines Press
582 Market Street, Suite 700
San Francisco, CA 94104
www.twolinespress.com
twolines@catranslation.org

This project is supported in part by an
award from the National Endowment for
the Arts.

ART WORKS.
arts.gov

Editor's note

*"Sometimes I write a wrong word on purpose, to savor
the tyrant's kick in secret."*
— Duo Yu, translated by Fiona Sze-Lorrain

What do we want the future of translation to be, and how do we guide it to that place? For this, our twenty-fifth anniversary issue of *Two Lines*, we invited six essayists and translators to wrestle with the future. For the most part, the questions are not new: Who gets translated, who does the translating, and what does "honoring" the original really mean? But the viewpoints and insights in this issue, I think, would have been unlikely even ten years ago.

Bonnie Chau, a second-generation Chinese American who had purposefully turned from her family's cultural history to be more "American," struggles in her essay with whether she even has the authority to translate from Chinese and what sort of "American" she is actually translating for. Madhu Kaza, in her essay, discusses her struggle not only to get literature from Telugu—a language with more speakers than Italian—published, but even to find access to study the language of her childhood in the United States. And ultimately, she discusses how broadening our idea of literature can give us clarity in unfamiliar (to Americans) political times.

I have been with *Two Lines* since Issue 16—half of the issues in the magazine's history. I don't know the future of translation, but I do know and am thankful that it will include new voices, like some of the translators in this very issue, and new perspectives on what translation looks like, what editing translation looks like, and what work gets published. As I think of how far literature in translation has come since *Two Lines* began in the early nineties, I'm incredibly optimistic about the complexity, diversity, and breadth of the art form's future.

Translation is an invitation, a bringing in of a reader who would be otherwise left outside. In the next twenty-five years I hope there will be many more homes we can be brought into, many more voices we can hear, and more translators, editors, and publishers supporting the bulky, beautiful machinery required to sit alone in a room and hear a voice speak to you alone from far away.

—CJ Evans

FICTION

Kwam Reunrom Hang Cheewit   26   The Attendant
DUANWAD PIMWANA   MUI POOPOKSAKUL

El día de cada día   52   Our Daily Day
ANNA LIDIA VEGA SEROVA   DAVID LISENBY

El cárabo   78   Screech Owl
SARA MESA   KATE WHITTEMORE

L'écrivain public   100   The Public Scribe
TAHAR BEN JELLOUN   RITA NEZAMI

Berenice (La resucitada)   118   Berenice (Risen from the Dead)
PEDRO LEMEBEL   MARGARET JULL COSTA

POETRY

Xi-yu   12   Drizzle
Xiang-cun-shi   14   Village History
Xiao-xia-lu   18   Leisure Summer Index
DUO YU   FIONA SZE-LORRAIN

Bu-yi man ki nemiayad   38   My Scent That Doesn't Pass
Dupin Detects   40   Dupin Detects
Mu'alaqa-i mah-i ru-yi   42   Song of the Moon Hanging over
dashtha-yi demeshq   the Fields of Damascus
BIJAN ELAHI   REBECCA GOULD AND
     KAYVAN TAHMASEBIAN

Jakby z rozpędu   60   As if with momentum
Krztyny   62   Not a scrap
Sen, w którym strzelasz   64   Dream in which you shoot
Kęsy   66   Mouthfuls
Wiele neonowych pętli   68   A bunch of neon nooses
JOANNA LECH   KAREN KOVACIK

In der Krängung   **70**   In the Heeling
KARLA REIMERT   PATTY NASH

Guirá dxi naa bacuzaguí   **88**   Every Day I'm a Firefly
Cada día soy luciérnaga
Pa Guiniu'   **90**   If You Say
Si Dices
"Pa ma nacaxhiiñilu'..."   **92**   "If a life springs within you..."
"Si en ti se gesta la vida..."
"Rarí qui rigaachisi gue'tu' ne ma'..."   **94**   "Here the dead don't just go to the
"Aquí los muertos no se entierran nomás   grave peacefully..."
y ya..."
IRMA PINEDA   WENDY CALL

"Når jeg har hørt de tomme rum i huse..."   **96**   "When I have heard the empty rooms
in houses..."
"When I have heard the empty rooms
of dwellings..."
"I aften skriver rusens blå Diana..."   **98**   "This evening's gentle high,
a blue Diana..."
"This evening writes euphoria's
blue Diana..."
INGER CHRISTENSEN   SUSANNA NIED AND
DENISE NEWMAN

Nafidha   **112**   A Window
Nafidhatan   **114**   Two Windows
Thalath Nawafidh   **116**   Three Windows
RA'AD ABDUL QADIR   MONA KAREEM

sami'tuhu yughannī   **126**   I Heard Him Singing
ḥajarun fī al-rīḥ   **128**   A Stone in the Wind
lasta shā'iran fī gharnāṭa   **130**   You Are Not a Poet in Granada
baladun yusammā al-ughniya   **132**   A Country Called Song
andalusiyyūn   **134**   Andalusians
NAJWAN DARWISH   KAREEM JAMES ABU-ZEID

ESSAYS: THE FUTURE OF TRANSLATION

138   Engaging the New Knowledge
MADHU H. KAZA

152   Silence, Exile, and Translating
BRADLEY SCHMIDT

162   Collaboration
HEATHER CLEARY

170   Writing the Reality We Want
LUCAS KLEIN AND ELEANOR GOODMAN

180   Impossible Connections
BONNIE CHAU

Contributors
198

Credits
203

Index by Language
205

THE

THE FUTURE OF TRANSLATION

Born in Shandong in 1973, national award-winning poet, essayist, and literary critic **DUO YU** cofounded the "Lower Body" poetry movement in the early 2000s. One of the signatories of the "Charter 08" manifesto that calls for political democratic reforms in China, he is still living under surveillance.

细雨

黎明。一只羊在雨中啃食绿荫。

梧桐低垂着，木槿花落了一地，满眼让人颤抖的绿

雨沙沙地落在园中，它讲的是何种外语？

一只红嘴的鸟儿，从树丛里飞出来，像一只可爱的手套

落在晾衣架上。

读了几页书，出来抽烟，天空低沉，云也和书里写的一样：

"他们漫步到黄昏，后面跟着他们的马……"

——然而一把刀！它滴着冰，有一副盲人的深瞳，盯着我。

一个人，要吞下多少光明，才会变得美好起来？

我拉起你的手——我们不被祝福，但有天使在歌唱。

一声哭的和弦，那是上帝带来的钟

在为我们称量稻米……

Drizzle

Dawn. In rain a goat chews tree shade.
Wutong trees droop, hibiscus is strewn everywhere, greenery
    a tremor floods the eyes.
Rain shuffles in the garden, what foreign language does
    it speak?
A red-beaked bird flies from the trees, like an adorable glove
that landed on a drying rack.
After reading a few pages, I come out for a cigarette. A grave
    sky, even clouds are as written:
They stroll until dusk, a horse trails behind...
—but a knife! It drips with ice: a blind man's deep pupils
    stare at me.
How much radiance must one swallow to feel wonderful?
I take your hand—we aren't blessed, but an angel sings.
A crying chord is a clock from God
to weigh rice crops for us...

L
I
N
E
S

乡村史

德宗三年，英军行于沪宁道上
湘乡薨，举人们忙于作挽联
王二忙于在小亚麻布衫里捉虱子……

……那秋日的雨，一直下到今天
一拨又一拨的愁云，仿佛秋天的心
风物冰凉，小流氓也感到无聊
庄家慵懒地长着，麦子躺在瓮里
张家的门紧闭，李家的狗
学会了沉思
一些人在廊下支起桌子，打牌
其中就有我死去多年的爷爷
闲暇贴在睫毛上，鞋子逸出了脚面
有人打太极摇扇子
有人读论语说废话
有人登高有人纳妾有人偷欢
偷到了心烦。还没到时间
还没到结党营社读水浒的时间
还没到磨刀自渎写密信的时间
还没到张灯佩剑孤独自饮的时间

Village History

In the third year of Guangxu's reign, British troops strolled
    along Shanghai-Nanjing Way
When Marquis Yiyong died, scholars busied themselves
    with elegiac couplets
Wang Er was busy catching lice in a sleeveless linen jacket...

...autumn rain from that day lasts until now
Depressing clouds chunk after chunk, like an autumn heart
Icy cold scenery: even little hooligans were feeling bored
Zhuang family grew sluggishly, wheat lay in urns
Zhang family's door was shut, Li family's dog
learned to contemplate
Some set up tables in the corridor and played mahjong
One of them was my Grandpa who died years ago
Leisure was pasted on their eyelashes, soles came out of
    their shoes
Someone practiced taiji and waved a fan
Someone read *The Analects* and talked nonsense
Someone mountaineered someone took in a concubine
    someone committed adultery
that lasted until it vexed them. It wasn't time yet
not time yet for *The Water Margin* or villains to unite and
    do harm
not time yet for honing knives and masturbating and
    writing secret messages
not time yet for lighting an oil lamp putting on an épée and
    drinking alone

还没到时间，雨水泡在雨水中
村长泡在寡妇家
粮食还在，灯绳还在，裤脚上的泥泞还在
民国远去了，还没到
重写的时间

T

W

O

not time yet, rain soaked in rain

The village chief dallied with a widow at her home

Food was still lying around, so were lamp cords, and mud on
      the ends of trouser legs

Gone and far was the Republican era, it wasn't time

yet for a rewrite

消夏录

上午写了两首诗，午睡醒来
感到面目可憎，皆删去
顿觉世界神清气爽。

*

一年也可当做三天过：新春、立夏、中秋
往往芒种一过，我就开始陷入混沌。

*

入夏以来，就很少写诗。
不写，其实也是一种写，每次小便
都在草书一个亡字。

*

我有时会在梦中杀人放火，白天遇到警察
还是会绕着走。

*

什么都不做时，感觉最忙，因此
我没有真正闲下来的时候。

Leisure Summer Index

After two morning poems, I wake up from a nap
feeling repulsive: delete everything.
The world feels refreshing out of the blue.

*

A year can be spent as three days: new spring, summer's
    prime, mid-autumn.
Usually, once past the ninth solar term, I start to plunge
    into chaos.

*

Ever since summer set in, I've written very few poems.
Not writing is a form of writing too: each time I urinate,
I write *perish* in cursive.

*

Sometimes I murder and set fire in dreams. When I bump
    into a policeman in the day,
I still take a detour.

*

Doing nothing feels busiest, therefore
I've never a real idle moment.

*

一个写小说的，写成了土豪劣绅
这也是没办法的事情——很多人一不小心
就有钱了。

*

有钱能使鬼推磨，推来推去的
有意思吗？

*

对我来说他世故得全无希望，
他总把落叶说成是二两铜钱。

T
W
O

*

我们在哪儿见过吗？三十之后
我基本就不记人脸了。

*

我有时故意把一个字写错，以体验
暴君的隐秘快感。

*

Through writing, a novelist has become a local mafia.
This can't be helped—many prosper
by accident.

*

With money one can do anything one desires—does grinding
        here and there
make any sense?

*

To me, he is so hopelessly worldly: in his words,
fallen leaves always sound like two copper coins.

*

Where have we met? After thirty years,
I basically can't recall faces.

*

Sometimes I write a wrong word on purpose, to savor
the tyrant's kick in secret.

*

生活就是一则四则运算，
得负数和无理数是常有的事。

*

读书，但很少读到结尾。我担心
每本书的结尾都潜伏着一个答案。

*

读完一本回忆录，突然发现
不会写诗了。还是平仄的路子好走。

T
W
O

*

讨厌他，就告诉他，这是一种美德。

*

这种事以后别再叫我，念诗就念诗
朗诵会都开始半个小时了，领导的话还没讲完
——我还没听说过有谁能领导诗人。

*

Life is but four arithmetic operations:
negative and irrational numbers are a common sight.

*

I read, but rarely to the end. I fear an end
in each book where an answer lurks.

*

Done with a memoir, I suddenly realize
I can't write poetry. Tone patterns work best.

*

Just tell him you hate him if you do: this is a virtue.

*

Don't call me after the event: a poetry reading isn't a big deal.
It's been half an hour since it began, yet the organizer isn't
    done with his introduction
—I haven't yet heard of anyone who can lead poets.

L
I
N
E
S

Duo Yu
Leisure Summer Index

*

装什么装？不生虱子才几天？为了反对一切
假正经，什么茶我都撮到一个壶里泡。

*

孤独时，就照照镜子，在一阵犬吠中
寻找韵脚。

*

我还是对自己太客气了，自己就像
自己的一个客人。

T
W
O

*

最近偏爱听雨，这是不是一种心灵上的腐朽？
中年之后，再指责自己就难了。

*

What's there to fake? Hasn't it just been a few days since you
     were rid of lice? To oppose everything,
pretend to be serious; I can press any tea into a pot and brew.

*

In solitude, look into a mirror; in the midst of dogs' barking,
seek metrical foot.

*

I'm still too polite to myself, myself
a guest to myself.

*

Lately, I've grown fond of listening to rain: is this a
     spiritual decay?
Past the middle years, self-criticism won't come easy.

L
I
N
E
S

DUANWAD PIMWANA is consistently regarded as an important female voice in contemporary Thai literature. A chronicler of women's lives and working-class realities, she is known for fusing touches of magical realism with social realism. She lives in the Thai east-coast province of Chonburi.

ความรื่นรมย์แห่งชีวิต

T
W
O

ยังเหลือเวลาอีกสามชั่วโมงผมจึงจะหลุดพ้น   เกรงว่าผมอาจจะรอให้ถึงเวลานั้นไม่ไหว ร่างกายอาจยุติการทำงานลงในนาทีอันใกล้นี้ นอกจากลูกนัยน์ตาที่กรอกขึ้นลงกับแขนและมือข้างขวาแล้ว   ผมยังไม่ได้ลองขยับส่วนอื่นๆ ของร่างกายมานานกว่าสองชั่วโมง ความจริงผมควรจะมาทำงานด้วยศีรษะกับแขนขวาข้างเดียวเท่านั้น ปล่อยให้ส่วนที่เหลือทั้งหมดได้ออกไปกระทำตามความปรารถนาของมันกับโลกภายนอก กระทำอย่างสาหัสสากรรจ์โดยเสรีด้วยความสามารถของอวัยวะแต่ละส่วน

ร่างกายของคนคนหนึ่งไม่อาจคงอยู่ได้โดยการนั่งนิ่งๆ อยู่ในพื้นที่แคบๆ ไปจนตลอดชีวิตหรอก   หัวใจที่เต้นอย่างอ่อนเนือยของผมบอกอย่างนั้น   ก็ในเมื่อผมมีขาที่เดินหรือวิ่งได้ไกลทีละหลายกิโลเมตร   แขนและมือของผมก็ทำอะไรได้ไม่รู้กี่หมื่นกี่พันอย่าง ดูน่าเศร้าไม่ใช่หรือที่จะปล่อยทิ้งมันไว้เฉยๆ ยังมีหูของผมอีก หูที่น่าสงสารของผม มันควรจะได้ยืนได้ฟังอะไรก็ตามที่มีความหมายมากกว่าคำสั่งเพียงสองพยางค์ที่ซ้ำไปซ้ำมา วนเวียนกันอยู่แต่เลขหนึ่งถึงเลขแปด... คำว่า ชั้นหนึ่ง ชั้นห้า ชั้นสี่ ชั้นเจ็ด คำเหล่านี้มีความหมายอยู่ในตัวมันเองเท่าขี้เล็บ และความหมายนั้นก็จบลงภายในเวลาไม่ถึงหนึ่งนาที หลังจากคำสั่งสองพยางค์นี้ หูของผมได้รับฟังแต่เรื่องราวที่พิกลพิการ บางครั้งไม่รู้ที่มา บางทีไม่รู้ว่าจะจบลงอย่างไร และบางคราวไม่รู้ทั้งตอนต้นและตอนจบ แต่ผมก็ได้ฟัง-- จำต้องฟัง ทำไมเล่า ในเมื่อผมควรจะได้ฟังในสิ่งที่ผมต้องการฟัง และมีสิทธิ์จะหลีกเลี่ยงจากเรื่องราวที่ไม่ต้องการรับรู้ เป็นความจริงหรือเป็นข้อเท็จจริงกันแน่ที่ผมมีสิทธิ์ แต่กลับไม่มีสิทธิ์

ในช่วงฤดูฝน หูของเราจะจับฟังเสียงลมพายุได้ไกลขนาดข้ามพื้นที่เป็นร้อยไร่ทีเดียว ป่าระกำคือต้นธารแห่งเสียง เป็นสัญญาณบอกให้รู้ล่วงหน้าว่าพายุกำลังจะมา นั่นเป็นช่วงที่ทำให้เราตื่นตัวและเข้มขึ้นเกลียวไปทุกขุมขน ความเหนื่อยล้าจากงานในไร่หายไปเป็นปลิดทิ้ง เราพากันวิ่งกลับบ้านอย่างไม่คิดชีวิต ขณะที่ผมกับน้องสาววิ่งแซงขึ้นหน้าไป แม่จะตะโกนไล่หลังมาว่าเมื่อถึงบ้านแล้วต้องเก็บต้องทำสิ่งไหนอย่างไร...

Translated by Mui Poopoksakul
Thai | Thailand

The Attendant

Three more hours remain before I'll be let out. I fear I won't be able to wait until then. My body might fail in the minutes to come. Other than my eyes, which glance up and down, and my right arm and hand, I haven't moved any other part of my body for over two hours. I should honestly show up for work with just my head and my right arm, leaving the rest of my body to go and do as it pleases in the outside world—do these things intensely, freely, to the best of its ability.

A body cannot survive sitting still in a confined area forever, so my limping heart tells me. Since I have legs capable of walking and running several kilometers at a time, and arms and hands fit to do tens or hundreds of thousands of things, isn't it a shame to leave them idle? And then there are my ears, my poor ears that should get to hear something, anything, with more significance than simple two-word commands, repeated over and over, bouncing only between numbers one and eight... The words "first floor," "fifth floor," "fourth floor," "seventh floor"—these words in and of themselves have as much meaning as the dirt under my nails, and that meaning is gone in the blink of an eye. Apart from these two-word instructions, my ears hear only deformed conversations, sometimes without a beginning, sometimes without an end, and sometimes without either. But I listen—I *have* to listen. And why is that, when I should be able to listen to what I want to listen to and have the right to avoid everything else? Is it true or an illusion that I have that right, a right that I've been deprived of?

L
I
N
E
S

During the monsoon season, our ears could pick up the sound of storm winds over a hundred *rais* away. The rustling of wild salacca leaves served as the vessel for the sound, sending a warning signal that a storm was coming. In that moment, we would be on high alert, tense down to every pore. We would sprint home as if there were no tomorrow, the fatigue from the day's work in the fields forgotten like it had been wrung out of our limbs. As my little sister and I would run ahead of the pack, our mother would yell from behind, telling us what to put away and do when we got home, and how. The house was far from the fields, but we would run without stopping. Each time, our parents probably prayed that the storm would bypass us or wouldn't be severe enough to blow the crops to the ground and cause damage. But my sister and I found it fun, although we would be dead tired. The wind might arrive first, followed by the rain, or they might arrive together at once, but not a single time did my sister and I ever reach our house before at least one of them hit, run as we did with all our might. Gray clouds would move swiftly from the west. Looking up, I used to think they resembled curtains being drawn over the sky. My sister liked to pretend that she was the one pulling the curtains. She would wait for the clouds to move a little ahead of us, and I would end up having to drag her along. The raindrops carried along by the storm winds were huge and fell with force. As they lashed down on us, we would feel the sting, urging us to run faster, until we arrived at our destination.

I desperately want to run. If I get to, I promise this run will be like no other in my life. I will pour all my energy into it, go as far as possible, as fast as possible, wearing myself out like never before, letting my mouth get so parched it tastes bitter. Every part of my body would join forces solely for this run. My arms would be rejuvenated, as well as my legs, my blood, and my heart. Every part of my body would come alive so that I could run, run on a path of my own choosing, run far and wide. I want to run without ever turning back. Please, don't let me run only to have to turn back. I'm not an elevator door that opens only to close again, nor am I an elevator user who steps in only to step out—oh, somebody help me, help me be able to run far and wide. Yes, it ought to be far *and* wide.

Space is tight in the elevator, too tight for running or even walking. In such a confined space, one is meant to stand. Considering its shape, the elevator is nothing more than a coffin for the living. People zip into the elevator, all of them with energy in their steps. I get a glimpse of them before they turn their bodies around behind me and face the doors, which close from both sides. Then they stand still and utter their two-word commands at my back. Lifting my right arm, I press the button of the requested floor and watch the green light move through the numbers, flashing upward, one, two, three, four, five, six, seven, eight; flashing downward, eight, seven, six, five, four, three, two, one. When the elevator doors open, the living humans step out and in. I get a quick look at them from the front, and a quick one from the back. The elevator doors shut, and then again come the commands, jabbing me in the back as I sit motionless in my chair, forcing my right hand to rise up and press… The more time passes, the more heavy-handed, and pointed, those two words become. When the voices dig into my back, I feel excruciating pain. Who could tolerate sitting still, allowing pain to be inflicted on them time and time again, endlessly? The living humans have no idea that they're hurting me. Of course the ones that do the hurting don't feel the pain; the victims are the ones that bear it. And how long do I have to wait until the former are the ones that suffer, so they will stop hurting me? Or do I have to turn into a baby chick before they realize what it's like to hurt somebody and end up being the ones in pain?

I knew that it was suffering, condemned to spin around like that, unable to stop. After wasting a lot of time, I discovered a way to help, which was to curl my index finger into the shape of a hook and grab it by the neck. But after some time, the symptoms would return—the twisted neck, the frozen eyes, the running in circles. The poor baby chick was attached to me, following me around constantly, and I don't know if what came to

L
I
N
E
S

pass was the chick's misfortune or mine.

The seizures the chick endured became less and less frequent, and I thought it would soon be cured. We were together all the time; I never let it out of my sight. So whenever its neck started to contort, right before it would start running in circles, I would rush over and grab its little neck with my hooked finger, a task I had to execute quickly if I wanted to prevent the symptoms from taking hold.

My chick was by my side even during meal times and when I went to the toilet. When I slept, it would huddle in a cardboard box next to me. When I went out to work in the fields, it would wander near my feet, constantly moving as they were, which meant that I nearly crushed it to death on several occasions. But there, like nothing and in the blink of an eye, its fate took an ill turn all over again. As I was swinging my hoe toward the ground, destiny whispered to the poor chick and summoned it under the blade. Its left leg and a bit of its wing were sacrificed to this cruel fate. My good intentions rebuffed, I felt frustrated and wondered why I had made any effort at all. I caught myself thinking: What was the point of this chick's existence? Its life was nothing but struggle; straight out of the eggshell, it was stricken with the strange seizure disorder. Its cries made me want to dig a grave and get it over with.

The following day, I went out to the fields without the chick. It stayed at home alone, withering in the cardboard box, where I'd left some rice and water in little cups. Out in the fields, I was in a foul mood, finding fault with everyone and everything. It didn't help that I felt tired and hot. My obligation to the chick, which wasn't supposed to have lasted much longer, was now getting dragged out. What was more, I didn't like having to take on a burden that reeked of pity like this. I had never felt so tired and hot as I did that day—these conditions make it so easy for abject thoughts to plant themselves in people's minds. I even resented my little sister, who was sitting in a classroom in comfort. When the sun was directly overhead, I headed home without waiting for anyone, vowing to myself that as soon as I washed my face and ate my lunch, I would reserve the bamboo daybed under the mango tree for myself straight through until two in the afternoon.

When I got home, I immediately heard a scraping noise. It persisted in frequent intervals as I stood there listening. Soon it occurred to me to go look in the cardboard box. The rice grains had spilled all over the place, and the entire bottom of the box was damp. The chick, neck crooked and eyes frozen wide, was struggling with its remaining leg to kick and scratch its way in a circle. I hooked my index finger around its neck, tending to it for a while before the seizure finally stopped. It let out a raspy cry and then lay still, eyes half shut, cradled in the palm of my hand. Its condition appeared to have worsened. I couldn't say how I felt in that moment, but I wondered for what purpose this chick had been born.

Under the mango tree, I lay back on the daybed, nestling the chick on my chest.

I was fed up... I wanted to kill it...but I pitied it.

I fell asleep for over an hour, instinctively waking up when it was time to go back to the fields for the afternoon. I sat up, completely forgetting that the chick could tumble off my chest. But in fact, it wasn't there. When I leaned over to look on the ground, I saw it lying there, its beak clamped onto the edge of a sheet of corrugated iron beneath the daybed, its body jerking so persistently that the sharp edge had sliced into the corners of its mouth. Its right leg was digging, leaving scratch marks on the ground. Four or five fire ants had found their way to its eyelids and the bleeding corners of its mouth. I looked at it for a short while and then got up and went inside the house. I picked out an old black work shirt too ratty to be worn. When I returned to the mango tree, the chick was in the same state as before. I spread the shirt out on the daybed, picked the chick up, brushed the ants off it, and carefully set it down on the cloth. Bending over, I observed the convulsing body up close and stared into the little eyes for a while before straightening myself up and folding one side of the shirt over the chick. I made a tight fist with my right hand and started counting, my eyes focused on the lump under the cloth; it twitched lightly,

L
I
N
E
S

a bit like a beating heart. Then I suddenly felt so depleted that I had to unclench my fist, peel the cloth open, and hook my finger around the chick's neck until its spasms stopped. Right then, my parents walked by, their path leading in my direction. They were already heading back out to the fields. My mother looked at me and smiled, amused. For the past few days I'd been so preoccupied with the chick that I must have seemed ridiculous. I watched my parents as they walked off into the sweltering sun. I would soon follow them.

I folded the cloth over again and pounded. The first time, a squeal snuck through. I pounded twice more, and then stopped—it appeared to be enough. I grabbed the bundle of cloth and headed for the fields, my hoe on my shoulder.

Who believes me when I say that I did it to put the chick out of its misery? I was the one suffering from having to lay hands on it. Isn't it twisted? When I hurt others, I'm the one that suffers; when others hurt me, I'm the one that suffers again. I stopped hurting others because I don't want to suffer anymore. But why do they continue hurting me? How long must I wait for them to stop?

None of the living humans want to go to the fourth floor, so I don't know what time it is or how much longer I have before I can escape. Other than looking up and down and raising my right arm and hand to press a button and then dropping them back down, I haven't attempted to move the other parts of my body to see if they still function. I should honestly come to work with only my head and my right arm. My legs are strong; my body is strong, a farmer's body built for physical labor. The world has farmers, and I'm a good farmer. But right now I'm an elevator attendant, even though such a job shouldn't exist in this world. Is it so troublesome to lift your hand up and press a button that they have to pass this task off to someone else, someone who could do so many other things? If I had been born with only a head and an index finger, this job would be suitable for me. It's a shame I'm really about to be left with only those two parts. The rest of me is slowly dying... Soon enough everything will probably end up the way it ought to.

But now I want to find out how long I have before I'm let out. The elevator opens on the first floor: I see the fried chicken stand, a kid stuffing a drumstick into his mouth... The elevator opens on the fifth floor: I see a shop girl resting her arm on a stack of bras, talking to a man... The elevator opens on the sixth floor: I see a group of middle-aged women sitting around a *suki* hotpot, sharing a good laugh as they lean in and ladle... The elevator opens on the eighth floor: I see a shop boy napping, draped over a loud speaker, and next to him three men standing there looking at televisions... The elevator opens on the seventh floor: I see the concession stand with popcorn and the cinema box office, but not a soul in sight... The elevator opens on the second floor: I see a young couple staring into each other's eyes over cups of coffee... The elevator opens on the third floor: I should see the girl behind the beverage counter, but a group of men is blocking my view... The elevator opens on the fourth floor—at last. I steal a look at one of the clocks in the timepiece store: in less than an hour, I will be free to go. But I haven't tried to wiggle the other parts of my body to see if they still work. I hope they haven't gone and died on me, especially when my heart hasn't stopped and is now begging to leave. I so painfully want to escape, to shoot out of this place like an arrow.

Only those completely ruined by exhaustion would want to sit still and not even move a finger. I would find no joy in such immobility unless my muscles burned with pain and my legs couldn't take another step. I've sat immobile for so long; I've sat in misery for too long, and I don't want to sit any longer. My heart is still beating, and I want to completely wear myself out—completely, not moderately or momentarily. It wouldn't be right to spend one's entire life idle and then mobilize only for a momentary burst of energy. It would make me happy to exert myself to the limit for as long as possible, and it would make me happier still to then rest for a short time.

L

I

N

E

S

I lugged a bushel of cassava roots on my shoulders, its weight bearing down on me. I could barely shuffle my feet, my legs feeling like they might give at any point, as I consoled myself with the fact that this was my last haul. When, finally, I reached the bottom of the wooden ramp leading up to the bed of the ten-wheeler truck, I rallied, trotting up the incline. The man I had to pass the bushel to was very high up because the cassava was piled past the top of the truck's grated wooden frame. I gathered whatever strength remained in me, bent a little at the knees, and thrust the bushel as far up as I could. As it was pulled from my hands, I felt as though all my energy had been hauled away with it, and I just let myself drop down from the ramp and collapse on the ground with the others.

One by one, we got up as the sun started to disappear. The bare land was strewn with scraps of tapioca plants. Large clumps of soil that had been dug up with the tubers were left upturned all over the fields. All of these cast long, neat shadows to the east. We scattered in different directions before daylight vanished, leaving the fully loaded truck quietly parked on that empty tract of land.

That evening a horn sounded from a distance. I bounded down from the house and ran toward the source of the honking, which was followed by the revving of an engine. As I stepped onto the road, waiting on the side, I spotted the cassava truck turning up from the top of the fields, and I could make out people's heads, appearing like dark shadows on top of the heaping mound of tubers. When the ten-wheeler drew near, the crew on top of the pile of roots leaned out to look at me and had a good laugh. I laughed back, realizing that I was the last to show up. But then instead of stopping, the driver accelerated, driving the truck right past me and kicking up a cloud of dust. I had my mouth open mid-laugh and nearly didn't get it closed in time, and I had to struggle to open my eyes. The others had a hoot at my expense. The truck parked about fifteen meters ahead. I stood there, trying to calm down, waiting until the dust had settled a bit before I walked over. Glancing down at my soiled shirt and pants, I wanted to cry. I didn't even have to think about my hair, which I'd made an effort to

T
W
O

wash and style with oil. When I reached the truck, I yelled at the driver, who was my foreman. He sat there shaking with laugher and refused to gratify me with a response. All I could do was climb on top of the cargo to join the rest of the crew. Seeing me up close, they laughed even harder. I'd gotten so dressed up, no wonder I was the last to show, one of them teased.

Hardly anything was visible now that dusk was upon us. The truck switched on its lights and set off once again. To make room, I dug out a small space in the mound of roots to lower myself into. I was still mad at the others for another half hour or so, but eventually I relented and started chatting and joking with them. Crawling along the bumpy dirt road, the truck took nearly an hour to reach a paved street. Even though it was dark by then, the air was still heavy with heat. Only when the truck had gained some speed and the breeze started blowing was it a pleasant ride up there.

As a child, I always dreamed of cruising on top of one of these heaping loads of tapioca roots. My mother and father and the other adults wouldn't let any of the kids sit there. Back then, I could only imagine what it would be like to sit so high up. Those lucky riders could probably see far into the distance and could tell where everybody's farm was all along the way. They could most likely see the roof of every house. Especially when I thought about the truck going fast, I could hardly wait... The day I was allowed to sit on top of the mountain of roots for the first time—I still remember vividly how my heart raced. I looked down over the side at my little sister, who was squirming in defiance as our father tried to shove her into the cab of the truck, where our mother was already seated. Even after I backed away to find myself a place to sit as our father climbed up, I could still hear her shrieking.

The air was starting to get cooler, and the stars in the sky were twinkling. Along both sides of the truck, there was only darkness. Only once in a while would we see lights flicker from inside isolated houses. When the breeze eventually made it too chilly, we dug away the tubers and slipped ourselves deeper among them, reclining. The roots' starchy aroma, intensified by their warmth, made for a cozy place to lie down. Now and

L
I
N
E
S

again I happily dozed off, until the truck reached the town. The bright lights woke us up instantly; wide-eyed, we immediately started looking around at all the shops and stylish people. When the truck stopped at a red light, the women strolling along the side of the road glanced at us, then turned their noses up and refused to look our way again. Together we hooted and hollered at them before the truck continued on its way. The city girls, how pretty and how slick they were. I used to wonder, if one of those ladies became my wife, would I be able to afford her wardrobe... Oh, how I wanted one of those smug beauties for my own, to hold close in bed every night.

We had to ride on top of the roots for nearly four hours straight, so our legs needed stretching when we climbed down at our destination. Our foreman stuck his head out, reminding us to be back at the agreed pick-up time, and then continued on alone with the truck to the sorting plant, where the roots would be sold. We were dumped in the center of town, beat as we were from the harvest, to make our own way to the local watering hole. Still, we walked over together in high spirits. Although I was stiff from being cooped up for so long, I felt happy.

It's practically time. The living humans are finished using the elevator. The other employees will start heading out soon. I still haven't attempted to operate the other parts of my body, and I want to understand why I'm not doing it so that I can get up and walk out. The time for my release has come. I haven't died and I can't sit still forever. It's funny to think that I was sliding up and down all the time. I hadn't remained in place but I hadn't moved, and despite that, I'm drained. It's time for me to eat. It's time for me to rest and sleep, to recharge my energy so that tomorrow I will have the strength to come back and sit still once again... Oh, no, this can't be. I must be mistaken—stories like this cannot really exist.

My heart is tired. If I wait any longer, it might stop altogether. By then I probably wouldn't wonder any longer whether or not I could move anything on my body other than my head and my right arm. If my heart were to give up, it would be pointless for the other parts of my body to continue to function. I probably wouldn't want to walk even if I could still do it. People want to walk or move with joy... Regardless, I have no choice but to check the other parts of my body.

With my heart dying a slow death, I try to move the rest of me. I struggle to stand even though I have no desire to get up. I step out with legs as stiff as logs. My body feels as if it's breaking apart. With extreme effort, I walk out. I can't stay here. My heart is dying, but this place is a coffin for the living; it isn't suited for my heart.

Thus I leave, even though I don't want to leave. I don't want to eat, don't want to sleep, don't want to sit still. Really, I should leave my heart and the other parts of my body here to die, and let my head and my right hand go back to eat and sleep, to relax, as compensation for the exhaustion they had to bear... Ah, that would be fair, wouldn't it?

L
I
N
E
S

BIJAN ELAHI (1945–2010) is the preeminent hermit-poet of Persian modernism. A major influence on the next generation of poets, his poetics is distinguished by a diversity of style and registers. His poems establish poetry as a vision experienced within the nuances of a language that constantly foreignizes itself.

بوی من که نمی‌آید

در این گنجنامه استعاره من باش ؛
بوی من که نمی‌آید ،
نظاره من به علف ، که استعاره می‌شود .

آنجا
تو بر سر شیری سنگی نشسته‌ای ،
و شیر که پایین نگاه می‌کند
به تپه‌ای آرام .

T
W
O

My Scent That Doesn't Pass

Be my metaphor in this inscription,
my scent that doesn't pass,
my gaze at the grass, that makes a metaphor.

There you sit
atop a stone lion.
The lion gazes calmly,
at the hill below.

L
I
N
E
S

Dupin Detects

آن یکی خال به پیشانی داشت ،
نقشه هم دقیق بود : حفره‌ای در سقف ...
و ماه در خسوف ...
هر دو تو آمده بودند ولی بعد فضای سفید بود ،
خیرگی شده بود از درون
یا بیرون ،
حتم نداریم وگرنه ساده‌تر می‌بود :
شاید برق جواهر بیرون
از حد تصور بود ، یا شاید
صاحبخانه غفلتا کلید چراغ را زده بود .
هر دزد ، به جا ، ثابت شد ،
صاحبخانه به جا و ثبوت این همه ، باری ، ثبوت نور شد
اینجا ، در این اتاق – با این اثاث ساده : یک میز
و روی قفسه
یک مجسمه شیوا –
در عکسی ،
نقطه شروع ردیابی‌ی ما ، سفید ، واقعا سفید سفید ...
و حتم نداریم که از نوردیدگی‌ست ،
که دوربین بی‌صاحب را
جای تاریکخانه در فضای نورانی
باز کرده‌اند ، یا از اصل
عکسی نگرفته بودند .

Dupin Detects

The other one had a spot on his forehead,
The plan was perfect: a hole through the ceiling...
and the moon in eclipse...
Both had broken in.
Then everywhere flashed white.
Dazzling, from without and within.
We are in doubt. Otherwise it would be simpler.
Perhaps the gem's dazzling
was beyond depicting, or perhaps
the landlord had turned on the light without warning.
Each thief's position was fixed.
The landlord was in place. All was fixed, fixed by light
here, in this room, so simply furnished: a table
and on the shelf,
a statue of Shiva.
In a picture,
at the beginning of our detection, white, absolutely white...
We are in doubt. Was it over-exposed?
Did they open
the damn camera up
in a lighted place instead of a darkroom,
or was no photo taken at all?

معلقه‌ی ماه روی دشت های دمشق

و دشت‌ها که سبزه می‌رویند
تا فراموش شوند ،
اما از سبزه دشت یاد می‌آید
ای فتا ، دشت‌های بی‌سبزه !

از چه این سوزش را
همیشه پنداری ؟. – ای ماه دمشق !
و نورست آخر
که می‌نشاند آتش را در
حریق جنگل‌ها . – عشق .

ستاره‌ی سحری
می‌داند کجا می‌انجامی .
می‌داند ، و نمی‌داند .

۸

رخ بیرون می‌گذاری از هر نیزار
گرچه ماه نیستی . –

و می‌شناسم حشراتی سیاه
که مهتاب می‌شوند ،
بس که می‌ترسند
ازمهتاب .

T
W
O

Song of the Moon Hanging over the Fields of Damascus

The fields grow grass
destined for oblivion.
And grass reminds you of the fields.
How generous are the grassless fields!

How do you assume your burning
will last forever, O Damascus moon?
At last, light
quenches the flames in
the wildfire. Love.

The morning star
knows where you end.
It knows and is ignorant.

8

You peep through each reed-bed.
Yet you are not the moon.

I am acquainted with black insects
that become the moonlight
for fear of
the moonlight.

L
I
N
E
S

۷

و سحر ، قله‌های تو را سرختر
کند ترس
که از هر چه داری و
از ترس خود نمی‌داری ...

که هوای هواست – که دم
درو نمی‌زنی و
در تو می‌زند –
آبی‌ی دوست‌داشتنی .

بیفتی
بلند شوی
و بهتت که می‌زند
دامنه‌هایم باشی .

۶

از نفسی
که حبس می‌کنم ، نه که غیبت تو
بدرخشد ..

چنینه می‌میرم
از زندگی ،
چنینه که بی آفتاب
روشنی ،

فیروزه‌ی رضا !

T
W
O

7

At dawn, your summit will turn scarlet
from your fear
from anything you have but
you don't have for fear...

Desire for air—that you don't breathe
in yet it breathes
in you—
is lovely blue.

You would fall.
You would rise.
And when amazed,
you would be my foothills.

6

Your absence does not shine
from the breath
that I hold.

I die like this—
alive.
Like this, sunless,
you are bright,

O Reza's turquoise!

۵

با این همه خواب نداری
شبی درازی و خواب نداری
روزی و آفتاب نداری ...

بی‌نیاز
تو بوده‌ای
نور چشم ! –
در آفتاب‌ها ...

با این همه باید یک بار
یک تشنگی بلد
بوده باشی ، یک بار
یک سراب ساخته باشی
وسط دریا .

۴

یک‌باره ترس برم داشت
افتاده باشی از سر دیوار ،
خم شدم بگیرم دیدم
خوشه خوشه آویخته‌ای .

بهار قدیم
خشک برآمد ،
با شکوفه‌ها
که در پرده‌های قدیم‌تر ماند و
اندکی چرک‌نما .

T
W
O

5

After all, you are sleepless.
You are a long night and sleepless.
You are a day and sunless...

You were
flourishing.
Light of my eyes!
In the sun...

After all, once you must
have known
a deep thirst, once.
You must have made a mirage,
in the middle of the sea.

4

All of a sudden, I was shocked with the fear of
you tumbling from the high wall.
I bent to catch you, but saw
you hanging on the bushes.

The old spring
burst up dry,
in blossoms
wrapped in older curtains and
a bit shabby.

L
I
N
E
S

۳

به آن یکی

شراره‌ها ، شراره‌ها :
این یکی خود آن یکیست .
آن یکی نیست این یکی .-
در شب ، که چنان برق برق می‌زند هر دم
که هر دم انگار نمی‌زند .

جوانی تو
مال علف‌هایی بود
که خش وخش می‌کردند و خواب نمی‌دیدند ...

T
W
O

اکنون رویا
پیرم می‌کند .

۲

Il orra le chant du
Patre tout la vie.
— Apollinaire

این ،
دستی که دراز می‌کنی ،
دست چوپانی‌ست
یا علف ایام ؟

رو به رو
می‌لمد در آفتاب
مرغ بادنما .

3

To That One

Sparks, sparks:
this one is that one—
that one cannot be this.
At night, when each moment shimmers so
much that it shimmers not at all.

Your youth
went to grasses
that rustled and dreamed not...

Now dreams
make me age.

2

*Il orra le chant du
Patre tout la vie.*
—Apollinaire

Here,
the hand you stretch—
is it a shepherd's hand
or the grass of days?

Over there,
the weathercock
lies in the sun.

به چرا ،
می‌روند و نمی‌رسند
سال‌های نوری ، که ندارند
نی‌نوازی در دنبال .

۱

آن وقت از بلاتکلیفی
در حفره چپ قلبم به چرت می‌افتی
تا تو را طبیعتی
سر راهی
بردارد .

درد
بی‌گمان تدریجی‌ست .-
یک روز
که در قبر کوچک بغلی
چمباتمه میزند

و یک سال
طول می‌کشد

T
W
O

Light years
go grazing and never arrive.
They have no piper
following them.

1

At that moment from idleness
you rest in the left chamber of my heart
until a creature passes
and picks you up,
as if you were an orphan.

The pain
is certainly gradual.
One day
it will squat
in the small neighboring grave

and remain
all year long.

L
I
N
E
S

ANNA LIDIA VEGA SEROVA (born in Leningrad in 1968) grew up between Cuba and the former Soviet Union, settling in Havana in 1989. "Our Daily Day," like much of her work, imaginatively portrays the physical experiences and emotional aspirations of characters coping with material hardship.

El día de cada día

A nosotras, que nos queremos tanto...

La sensación de estar dando cabezazos contra una pared. Tal vez has visto cómo otras personas la atravesaron sin el menor esfuerzo e intentas imitarlas y chocas y vuelves a chocar. Mi amiga Beba tiene la frente rota de tanto golpear el concreto. Cualquier día de estos le descubren un cáncer en el cerebro, la masa enceláfica hecha un revoltillo. Por las noches hay que ponerle compresas frías de manzanilla u otra hierba medicinal para que baje la inflamación. Ella cierra los ojos, intenta dormirse, pensar que resbala nadando al fondo del océano. Hay una luz allá en el fondo. Sabe que cuando llegue a esa luz estará dormida, pero en la mañana no recordará si fue un cocuyo, un farol o una estrella. A la mañana, la brutal certeza de que todo vuelve a comenzar.

Todo vuelve a comenzar. No hay comida, no hay dinero, no hay ropa limpia, no hay detergente para lavar la sucia, no hay jabón para bañarse, no hay champú, no hay pasta de dientes... ¿Para qué quieres cepillarte los dientes si no hay comida? No hay dinero, no hay, no hay, no...

Mi amiga Beba se mira los ojos en el espejo. Hermosos ojos. Busca una respuesta como una luz en el fondo del océano, pero no hay cocuyos, no hay faroles, no hay estrellas. No hay. ¿Qué hace la gente para tener hermosos ojos y boca y pelo a pesar de que no hay champú? ¿Qué hace la gente? Se pasa las manos por el cuello, hermoso cuello, y tetas, y barriga. ¿Qué hace? Se vira y observa su espalda en el espejo. Hermosa espalda, hermoso culo…

Translated by David Lisenby
Spanish | Cuba

Our Daily Day

To us, who love each other deeply...

The feeling of banging your head against a wall. Maybe you've seen how others passed through without the slightest effort, and you try to follow, and you hit it, and you hit it again. My friend Beba has a broken forehead from so much smashing concrete. Any day now they'll discover she has brain cancer, her cerebral tissue totally scrambled. At night she has to apply cold compresses with chamomile or some other medicinal herb so the inflammation will go down. She closes her eyes, tries to fall asleep, to imagine she's swimming, slipping into the depths of the ocean. There's a light down there in the depths. She knows that when she gets to that light she'll be asleep, but in the morning she won't remember if it was a firefly, a streetlight, or a star. In the morning, the brutal certainty that everything is starting over again.

Everything is starting over again. There's no food, no money, no clean clothes, no detergent to wash the dirties, no soap to shower, no shampoo, no toothpaste... What do you want to brush your teeth for if there's no food? There's no money, there's no..., no...

My friend Beba looks at her eyes in the mirror. Beautiful eyes. She looks for an answer like a light in the depths of the ocean, but there aren't any fireflies, there aren't any streetlights, there aren't any stars. There aren't any. What do people do to have beautiful eyes and mouth and hair even though there's no shampoo? What do people do? She brushes her hands over her neck, her beautiful neck and breasts and belly. What do they do? She turns and observes her back in the mirror. Beautiful back, beautiful ass. Sell their ass! What else are they going to do?

My friend Beba looks for the cleanest clothes among the dirties. She has a friend that might have a few pesos; maybe he'll buy her ass for a few pesos. In reality, he's not a friend, more like an acquaintance. Syrupy gaze, drooling mouth, forgettable name, Pupo or Tato, an acquaintance of mine too, of course.

The feeling that with each step forward you take another one back. Like a stupid puppet dance. Pupo or Tato has swollen ankles from so much marching in place. At night he's supposed to soak his feet in a washtub with lukewarm water and salt. Any day now they'll have to put both his legs in casts, and he'll go around hopping: tak, tak, with his crutches. (He also might break his legs falling from a cliff he tried to climb, or in an ordinary traffic accident while riding his brand new mountain bike.)

Pupo or Tato looks out the window. Out there people are walking, all those happy people, beautiful women, none of them his. What do people do to have one? He goes hopping all the way to bed: tak, tak, with his crutches. He lies down, looks at the ceiling. He has pinned-up pictures of movie stars on the ceiling, beautiful women, none of them his. What do people do? He also has some porn pictures: billowing breasts, vulvas spread open, none of them his. What do they do? Tak, tak, it starts to rain. Nothing. What is he going to do? Wait for a stroke of luck, a divine appearance... Tak, tak, someone knocks on his door.

Pupo or Tato hurries to open it, hopping along, tak, tak, with his crutches, he can't make himself believe it, it can't be real, a divine appearance, a stroke of luck, a woman: my friend Beba.

Come in, you're all wet, I'll get you a towel, tak, tak, take this pink one, later I'll hang it in a frame over my bed, next to the pictures; do you want to see my stamp collection? my CD collection? my brand new mountain bike? I've waited so long for this moment...!

My friend Beba has little experience in the art of selling her ass. She starts by talking around the subject: there's no food, she says, there's no money. Pupo looks at her beautiful eyes, Tato breathes her magic scent even though there's no soap, there's no deodorant. You'll be the queen of this house, you'll have it all.

Ok, she says, get started. He pulls out his cock, he spits into his hand, rubs it. Can I get it up for you? She takes off her clothes, the cleanest of her dirties, she touches herself; there you go, he says, that's good.

Tak, tak, the rain. Tato, facing the ceiling, doesn't see the pictures of movie stars, the porn pictures. Tak, tak, the bed springs. Pupo looks at the woman's eyes and imagines he sees a light there in the depths. Tak, tak, her ass against his thighs. I love you, he says, I'm happy. How little it takes to be happy. Yes, she says, keep going. Tak, tak. It's a pain to do it with both legs in casts. My friend Beba's wet hairs, her moist skin, and that magic scent owing to the lack of shampoo, deodorant, soap. Billowing breasts, my friend Beba's vulva spread open, beautiful eyes, her eyelashes, tak, tak. The light closer and closer. A firefly? Wait, he says. A streetlight? His release sprays her wildly, tak, tak, it rains down on her belly and her breasts and her beautiful neck, tak, tak, it spatters her face... Definitely, it was a star.

I'm happy, he repeats, syrupy gaze, drooling mouth. You'll be the queen of this house, you make me so happy...

I don't want to be queen. I need money. A few pesos...

For you I'd do anything. Sell my stamp collection, my CD collection, my brand new mountain bike... We'll get married next week. No, this week is better. Does Thursday sound good?

My friend Beba cleans herself with the pink towel that's now less pink. I need money, a few pesos. She starts to get dressed, to put on the cleanest of her dirties that are now less clean.

There's no food...

Are you hungry? I can make you tea...

Bye, see you when you sell your bike.

Tomorrow for sure! At the latest, the day after... I love you. I'll always love you.

Tak, tak, the rain against the window.

My friend Beba walks between the puddles, slowly, slowly, as if she doesn't ever want to get back home. She thinks about her friend Helena, the whole time she's been thinking about her friend Helena, at no time has she stopped thinking. About her friend Helena's embrace, about her silent eyes and her look of resignation. Her friend Helena (who is me, to be exact) waits for her at home, waits for her to arrive with a few pesos, there at home.

The feeling of falling down a bottomless pit. The deeper it gets, the darker, the darker it gets, the quieter. Helena (who is me) has forgotten the words, has become a fish. She feels like some time ago her heart and her guts came out of her mouth and stayed floating up above, at the surface of the pit, together with all the words in the world. Any day now she'll hit bottom, where there's no light of any kind, and she'll smash against the rocks. I, fish without a heart, receive my friend with the most innocent expression I can manage to unfold. You took a while, I say, as if she had gone to the corner to buy cigarettes. How'd it go? Beba shrugs her shoulders, fills the bucket with water. I'm dirty. I want to take a bath. Well, continues Helena (me) in her most natural tone, while you bathe, I'll make a little tea. Are you hungry? Beba shrugs her shoulders. Yes, a little. It's like playing house. I bang the pots and pans in the kitchen, loudly.

I'm clean now. Do I look clean? She comes out naked, water dripping from her hair and her eyelashes. She looks the same, probably because there's no soap. You're gorgeous, I want to tell her, you're the most beautiful woman on Earth, I want to tell her, but I don't say it. My voice keeps bobbing at the surface of the pit while I keep descending imperceptibly.

Do you want to tell me about it? I hear my voice ask. No, answers Beba, and tells everything. Or, if not everything, at least part of the things, a large part. After, she closes her eyes, tries to fall asleep. She imagines she's swimming, slipping into the depths of the ocean. But there's no light down there in the depths. Her ocean has been left without fireflies, as if it were the pit of the disheartened. It's been left without streetlights or stars, and the deeper it gets, the darker, and the darker it gets, the quieter.

I embrace my friend Beba, and I sing her a sorrowful lullaby. Most lullabies are sorrowful. I'd like to have a brand new mountain bike to take you out for a ride. Take you far, very far, to a place where it never rains, where no one cries: tak, tak, tears on the pillow. If I had a brand new mountain bike, I'd put you on the rack and go around the entire city pedaling happily while the wind tousles your beautiful hair despite the lack of shampoo. If I had a bike, I'd cross the entire island with you, and people would come out to greet us, and they'd throw us flowers. They'd wait for us at town entrances with their municipal bands, and they'd bid us farewell with banners; poets would write lines to us, and troubadours, songs. If I had a bike, I would lay it at your feet as an offering, as a sublime token of my love, and we would make love over it. But I don't have it, I don't have a bike, I don't have a mountain bike, a brand new mountain bike. What do people do to have one? I watch my friend Beba sleeping, so close and so out of reach. I don't have anything to give her. What do people do? What do they do?

Selling your ass can turn into an obsession. Putting ads in the paper (Ass for sale / two available / good condition / reasonable price / offers accepted / for more information call 66–oo–oo), printing flyers and sticking them on all the telephone poles, at markets, on bus stops and fences. Making one spot for radio and another for television. Using suggestive images of the advertised merchandise (never showing it completely to achieve greater impact). Selling a bike also can turn into an obsession. Being known in the neighborhood (and outside of it) as the bicycle imbecile. Tossing it onto your shoulder so as not to harm its brand new tires, and moving along, tak, tak, hopping up and down on your crutches. Stopping in places with the most black market activity, offering it at a ridiculous price in comparison to its real price (it's priceless), hawking it artistically, hinting at discounts, insisting, failing, insisting again and failing again, one step forward, one step back, a stupid puppet dance.

We have food, we have clothing and detergent to wash the clothes, and soap, shampoo, deodorant, toothpaste, and perfume. We have a few pesos, there's always someone dropping a few pesos out an ass or two. We have a few pesos, but not enough. It's never enough. It still doesn't cover the cost of a brand-new mountain bike.

We should stop, my friend Beba says from time to time, with a dim look in her beautiful eyes. Her whole forehead is broken from smashing the concrete. Her whole ass broken too. At night she has to apply cold compresses with chamomile or some other medicinal herb so the inflammation will go down.

I can't, Helena responds and embraces her, I can't stop. She continues her free fall, there's no one to stop her. Any day now she'll hit bottom and smash against the rocks.

From time to time I run into Pupo, syrupy gaze, drooling mouth, with his bike on his shoulder: tak, tak, hopping along on his way to the market. When? I ask him. That's my whole life, says Tato, it's my heart. I shrug my shoulders. Some time ago my heart came out of my mouth and stayed floating at the surface of the pit, there up above, where very faintly shines a light that might be a firefly, a streetlight, or a star.

In the morning, the brutal certainty that everything is starting over again.

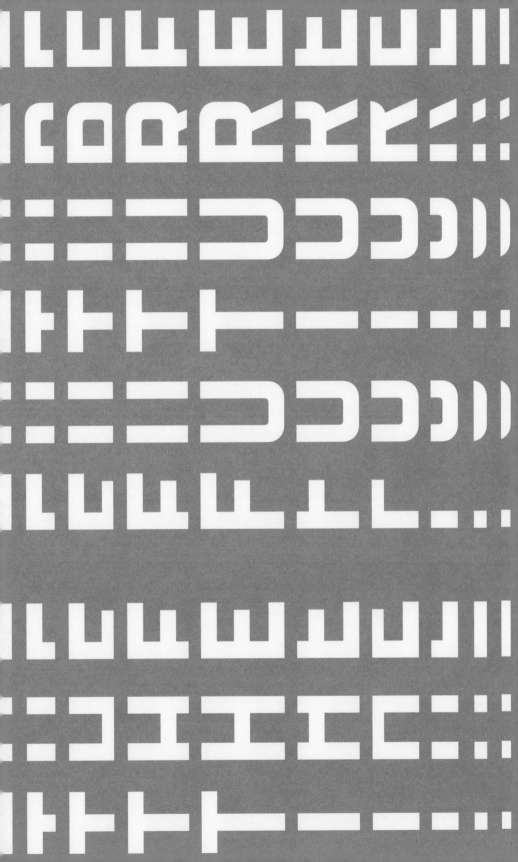

JOANNA LECH (born in 1984) is the author of five collections of poetry, most recently *Piosenki piknierów* (Songs of Picknickers), and the novel *Sztuczki* (Tricks). Her work draws influences from other cultures, and these poems connect to a playlist of songs. Lech lives and works in Krakow.

Jakby z rozpędu

Berlitz
—Seam

W spektaklu tym odgrywam wszystkie role, kolejno
ściągam słuchawki, ociekam żywicą i mówię o deszczu.
Stoję tak nieruchomo, jakbym parzyła, mówię o deszczu,
bo jestem rzeką, mówię, że upał, bo lepisz się do mnie
oczami, ale nocą, mówiłeś, śniło ci się, jak wyłam.

I to, jak wbijałam gwoździe w śliwki (kamieniem).
Klęczałam na śniegu, chciałam wyssać ci szpik (z łopatek)
(chciałbyś) (z łopatek czy z bioder?) Zataczałam łuki
w powietrzu (rękami?) i wyłam. Zagrażałam światu.

T
W
O

As if with momentum

Berlitz
—Seam

In this performance I play all the roles, one by one
I slip off ear buds, drizzle sap, and talk of rain.
I stand so still as if I were steaming, and talk of rain,
'cause I'm a river, I say, in a heatwave, and your eyes
    keep sticking
to mine, but at night, you say, in your dream I was howling.

And I pounded nails in plums (with a stone). On my knees
in the snow, I wanted to suck out the marrow (from
    your shoulders)
(you liked that) (though from the shoulders or your
    hips?) I traced
arcs in the air (and howled). And threatened the world.

LINES

Krztyny

Sunday
— Sonic Youth

Dziś jednak uciekam. Słyszę szum kropel
na trawie i nie ma we mnie ni krztyny spokoju.
Natychmiast chciałabym nie żyć albo bawić się
w chowanego w twojej wielkiej, dusznej głowie.
Pocąc się w deszczu, chciałabym wyjechać.
Kraść samochody w Meksyku, robić tatuaże
dziewczynom z Saint-Tropez. I żeby były
te wąskie, niebieskie korale na przegubach
ich dłoni i żeby był przeciąg.

T
W
O

Not a scrap

Sunday
—Sonic Youth

This is the day I escape. I hear drops hiss
on the grass, and there's not a scrap of peace in me.
Just like that I want to die or play
hide and seek in your big, muggy head.
Sweating in the rain, I want to run off somewhere.
Steal cars in Mexico, ink tats on girls
in Saint-Tropez. Let sheer blue beads
ring the hinges of their wrists
so that a breeze wafts through.

L
I
N
E
S

Sen, w którym strzelasz

If you stayed over
—Bonobo

do kaczek, skrzelami. W tej czapce
z pomponem, co tak śmiesznie dyndał
na święta. Hej, wejt! Gdy pociągasz
za spust, pęka mi głowa.

Masz długie palce i przerwę między zębami.
W upale pocisz się bardzo i gdy pociągasz
za spust, strzela mi w stopie. Hej,

wejt! Rybie haczyki brzęczą w kartonie.
Sen, w którym strzelasz do mnie palcami
i gdy się uśmiechasz, w tej przerwie

jest ogień.

T
W
O

Dream in which you shoot

If you stayed over
—Bonobo

at ducks with your gills. In that stocking cap
with the silly pompom dangling
like Santa's. Hey, wait! When you pull
the trigger, my head explodes.

You have long fingers and a gap between your teeth.
In this heatwave you sweat a lot and when you pull
the trigger, I feel my feet pop. Hey,

wait! Fish hooks clatter in the tackle.
I dream you shoot me with your fingers
and when you smile, in that gap

there's fire.

L
I
N
E
S

Kęsy

Się ściemnia
— Maanam

Gdzieś zaczyna się burza. Ale tu wciąż
możemy złapać trochę szklistego oddechu.
Spod dywanu pulsuje techno, ściemnia się
i moje serce jest czarne jak dłonie palacza.
Przysypiam i już się nie mogę oderwać
od tych splotów, rozrzuconych gałązek
i sęków. Żeby nie zapomnieć, robię zdjęcie

T   kotu i żeby nie pamiętać, skaczę z okna
W   w sam środek. Rosa, myślę, trawnik
O   w błękicie. Myślę, koniec świta, kipisz.

Translated by Karen Kovacik
Polish | Poland

Mouthfuls

It's getting dark
—Maanam

Somewhere a storm's brewing. But here
we can still catch a bit of glassy air.
Techno's pulsing under the rug, it's getting dark,
and my heart is black as a smoker's hand.
I'm nodding off but can't get free
of these tangles, scattered branches
and knots. So as not to forget, I take pics of the cat.
So as not to remember, I jump from the ledge
in the midst of it all. I sense dew, the lawn
gone blue. I think: the end is clear.

L
I
N
E
S

Wiele neonowych pętli

Dead radio
— Rowland S. Howard

Dziś znowu widziałam, jak zataczałeś się po ulicy.
Zobaczyłam cię w chłopcu, gapiącym się na mnie
w tramwaju. Miał podobną koszulkę, co ty
miałeś wczoraj i chciałam wykroić mu oczy.

Ale w kieszeni nie miałam nawet chusteczki.
I tłum, w który uciekłam, zdawał mi się jeziorem.

(Poszłam za tym blondynem, bo wyglądał trochę jak ty.
Dostał to, co miałam dla ciebie, ale ty też usłyszałeś
trochę z tego, co miałam do niego, więc po czasie myślę,
że jesteście kwita).

A dopiero, co wczoraj znalazłam twój włos i chciałam
go połknąć. Ale położyłam pod poduszkę, zasnęłam z nożem
w zębach, był świt i prowadziłeś mnie na tym sznurku
prosto w zamieć. Jak w błogi, blady lęk.

Translated by Karen Kovacik
Polish | Poland

A bunch of neon nooses

Dead radio
—Rowland S. Howard

Today I saw you stagger through the streets again.
A guy staring at me in the tram reminded me
of you. His shirt looked like the one you had on
yesterday, and I wanted to cut his eyes out.

But I didn't even have a tissue in my pocket.
And the crowd I fled into felt like a lake.

(*I followed that blond guy because he looked a bit like you.*
He got what I had for you, but you also heard
a bit of what I had for him, so now I'm thinking
you guys are even.)

And only yesterday I found a hair of yours and wanted
to swallow it. But I put it under my pillow, fell asleep
    with a knife
in my teeth. It was dawn and you led me on a rope
right into a blizzard. Into that sweet, white dread.

KARLA REIMERT is a German poet. *Picknick mit Schwarzen Bienen* (Picnic with black bees), excerpted here, was published in 2014 and was named best debut by the Berlin Literaturwerstatt that same year. Reimert has won the Würth Poetry Prize, the Rheinsberg Author Forum Prize, and the Essay Prize for the Japanese Consulate.

In der Krängung

VIII

Mutter schenkt mir ein Tagebuch.
Ich fülle es bis zum Abendessen.

Biotope, darin Katzen und Amseln,
die sich gegenseitig zu Tode jagen.

Ich übe mich in Gerechtigkeit und Butterbroten.
Kein Tier darf hungrig fliehen.

Ich zeichne: schwarzes Glas, grünes Fell.
Tiere mit riesigen knorpeligen Zungen.

Später weißes Fleisch, rote Striemen.
Das Beste an Wunden: wie gefährlich sie sind.

T
W
O

In the Heeling

VIII

Mother gives me a diary.
I finish it by dinner.

Biotopes with cats and blackbirds,
hounding each other to death.

I practice in justice and buttered bread.
No beast should go hungry.

I draw: black grass, green pelt.
Beasts with giant, gristled tongues.

Later white meat, red striations.
What's best about wounds: how they're dangerous.

IX

Meine Angst ist eine Jägerin.
Sehr wach liege ich inmitten der Meute.

Komm rüber, rufen die Flügelwesen,
wir reiten hinunter zum Fjord,

im feuchten Hafer Totemtiere jagen.
Riesige Wildschweine folgen uns auf dem Fuß,

im Unterholz lauert Lust auf Beute und Tribut.
Sobald der Bogen bricht, befehle ich den Angriff.

T
W
O

IX

My fear is a huntress.
Keen and awake, I lie in the pack.

Come here—flights call—
we're off to the Fjord,

hunting totems in moist oats.
Giant boars tail us on foot,

lust for loot and tribute lurks in the thicket.
I order strike once the bow breaks.

L
I
N
E
S

XII

Sommer. Ich liege in Leere. Eine Puppe.
Höre Mutter weinen.

Die Stimme meines Vaters, Mutters Namen
wie Kämme durch ihre Tränen ziehend.

Durch die Türritzen
kriechen Kränkungen.

Vorm Fenster Nachtlicht, durchstoßen von Blättern.
Schlaf, aufgeworfen im Zickzack,

Wände, wo Schatten Schatten jagen.
Ich liege in dünnster Decke.

T
W
O

Wenn Mutter weint, zittert mein Hirnlappen.
Meine Haut erhöht ihre Spannkraft, wird puppig.

Nur die zarte Kehle unter meinen Knien
bittet um Wunden.

XII

Summer. I lie in oblivion. A doll.
Hear Mother cry.

The voice of my father, Mother's name
pulling through her tears like a comb.

Ignominy crawls in
through cracks in the door.

Nightlight at the window, pierced with leaves.
Sleep, raised in zigzag,

walls, where shadows hunt
shadows. I lie in the skinniest spread.

My lobe quivers when Mother cries.
My dollskin augments its tone, cocoon softens,

only the tender hollows of my knees
beg for wounds.

L
I
N
E
S

XIII

Aus Mitgefühl verrate ich Mutter
die Namen meiner Tiere:

eines das rudert, eines das segelt,
eines, das in der Krängung liegt.

Mutter schenkt mir ein Gefieder zum Trost.
Ich drehe mich damit vorm Spiegel.

Was soll das sein?
Ein Schwarzmarktgeschäft?
Eine psychiatrische Initiation?

T
W
O

Wenn ich Mutters Gefieder trage,
werde ich ein Flügelwesen.

Ich bin gefährlich für mich.

XIII

Of compassion, I reveal
my animals' names to Mother:

one that sculls, one that sails,
one that lies in the heeling.

Mother gives plumage to comfort me.
With it, I pirouette in the mirror.

What's this?
A black-market deal?
A psychiatric initiation?

When I wear Mother's plumage
I become a winged thing.

I am dangerous to myself.

L
I
N
E
S

SARA MESA is considered one of the most notable voices in contemporary Spanish narrative. Described as intimate and unsettling, her work approaches themes of power and freedom in language that is taut, tense, and unadorned. She lives in Seville.

El cárabo

T
W
O

La chica volvió la cabeza desde lo alto de la loma y los vio a todos alrededor de la mesa de pícnic. En la distancia, la conversación era un murmullo ininteligible, como un zumbar de abejas. El sol estaba cayendo y la luz se retiraba de los pinos revelando verdes oscuros y cavidades que habían permanecido ocultas todo el día. Olfateó el aire—tierra húmeda, lavanda y romero, una mierda de vaca aplastada por la rueda de un coche—y regresó con los demás, demorándose en cada paso. El chasquido de las agujas de pino que se quebraron bajo sus pies se fue debilitando al acercarse, asfixiado por la voz de la tía, una voz como salida de una tinaja, grave, poderosa, pétrea. Todos apuraban los restos de la merienda en torno a ella, pidiendo su consentimiento, esperando su turno con una medida escrupulosidad. La tía sabía siempre qué había que hacer y los pasos que había que seguir para hacerlo. Sin permitir que nadie alterara su ritual, había administrado con lentitud la mantequilla, el foie gras, las rebanadas de pan tostado y el café con leche. Actuaba sin prisa, como si el tiempo también estuviese obligado a amoldarse a su ritmo. Sus palabras ocupaban toda la explanada y se expandían más allá de las suaves colinas terrosas. La chica se detuvo a observarla a unos metros. Aquel día cumplía veintidós años y ésa era toda la celebración que le estaba permitida: pinares, coches, merienda campestre y un encuentro familiar con viejos amigos que ni siquiera eran los suyos.

A un lado, metido en uno de los coches, el tío se cortaba las uñas de los pies con las flacas piernas extendidas fuera de la puerta. En la rigidez de su mandíbula había una concentración casi religiosa. . . .

Screech Owl

At the top of the hill the girl turned and saw the others around the picnic table. From a distance, the conversation was an unintelligible murmur, like the buzzing of bees. The sun was setting and light was vanishing from the pines, revealing dark greens and hollows that had remained hidden during the day. She breathed in the air—damp earth, lavender and rosemary, cow shit flattened by a car tire—and returned to the others, dragging her feet. The snap of the pine needles breaking beneath her steps grew weaker as she drew near, drowned out by the voice of the aunt, a voice like from the depths of an earthen jar, deep, strong, stony. The others gathered around her, eating the last bits of supper, seeking her permission, waiting their turn to be served with restrained scrupulousness. The aunt always knew exactly what had to be done and the proper steps to do it. She slowly dished out the butter, the *foie gras*, the slices of toasted bread, and the *café con leche*, allowing no one to disturb her ritual. She performed deliberately, unhurried, as if time itself was obliged to mold to her pace. Her words filled the esplanade and extended beyond the smooth boggy hills. The girl stopped to watch her from a few yards away. It was her twenty-second birthday and this was all the celebration they granted her: the pine forest, a car ride, a picnic in the countryside, a family gathering with old friends that weren't even hers.

Off to the side in one of the cars, the uncle was clipping his toenails, his skinny legs hanging out the door, an almost religious concentration in the rigid set of his jaw.

"Time to start packing up," he said when he'd finished, looking at the horizon. "It's getting dark."

He tucked the clippers in his shirt pocket and turned his tired eyes to the table. The aunt continued speaking as if she hadn't heard. Her speech—clipped, abrupt—did not allow for interruptions. She had extremely fine wrinkles above her lip; from a distance, they gave the impression of a very sparse but soldierly mustache.

"These days everybody talks about solidarity and commitment and there are thousands of campaigns and protests and petitions for some cause or another. But you have to take care of your own first, right? Helping other people, people that are far away, bah, that's too easy. Give to charity? Send old clothes to Africa? Sponsor a kid? No merit in any of it. What *is* hard is being there, every second, for your own people. Looking out for them, not letting them down. Teaching them to carry on, keeping them from getting lost or off track. Now that's helping, the rest doesn't count."

The couple sitting next to her—a thick bosomy redhead and her husband, small and reserved—listened and chewed. They'd been the aunt and uncle's neighbors for many years and were familiar with her ways. They kept their mouths closed and showed their agreement with slight movements of their heads. A boy of six or so sat a little ways away. He was dark-haired, freckled, lost in thought, an absorbed look on his impassive face. He ate his toasted baguette indifferently, throwing away the burnt edges of the bread. The redhead admonished him with a wink, but the aunt caught on immediately.

"Oh, come on! Eat nicely, would you? You'll be skin and bones if you carry on like that! Don't play with your food!"

She changed her tone and turned to the redhead, narrowing her eyes. She emphasized certain words, as if merely uttering them disgusted her. If it were up to him, he'd eat nothing but *junk*. Parents these days don't make any effort. A nice *tostada* for an afternoon snack? Oh no, that's *old-fashioned*! A donut or slice of pizza is *so* much better. His mother pays no attention to him. Typical of that part of the family, it must be genetic. They have their babies young and then *abandon* them. We raised this one, too," she added, nodding toward the boy.

The boy watched his mother closely as she continued to make her way down the hill, staring at the toes of her shoes. The girl looked up and smiled at him weakly. He stood up, his growing body skinny and awkward, and with the toast still in hand, approached the uncle, who was putting out the last embers of the campfire. A few coals still burned among the charred logs. The man threw fistfuls of earth on them, taking care not to dirty himself. A magpie flew overhead, the sound of its caw suspended in the air.

"Silvio isn't here," the boy announced.

The aunt looked at him, eyes blazing. The boy flushed. His freckles stood out even more against his skin.

"Where is he?" she shrieked.

No one knew how to respond. They had already folded up the table, loaded the cars, put the trash in bags. The uncle closed the boot of the Fiat and rubbed his hands together. They'd have to take a look around, he said looking at the sky. Pink and mauve clouds broke apart, admitting the last rays of light. An inhospitable dampness rose from the ground.

"*A look around?* Doesn't he know what time it is? What's that nephew of yours thinking?"

The redhead tried to calm her. He must have gotten distracted, that was all. Silvio knew the countryside well, her husband observed from off to the side, stepping on the smoking remnants of the fire. He wasn't a kid anymore, he wasn't going to get lost.

"I know he's not going to get lost! But we can't wait for him forever! We have to go!"

The boy looked around and in a soft voice suggested that they call his mobile. Call his mobile! the aunt brayed. Everyone knew they didn't have service there. The neighbors looked at her for a moment, unsettled, unsure of what to do. The uncle opened the boot again and busied himself rearranging the bags. The aunt threw a shawl over her shoulders, as if all the cold in the air had suddenly descended on her alone, scowled, and continued to mutter without taking her eyes off the path.

"I'll go look for him, *tía*," the girl said. "I'll take the boy."

She didn't wait for permission. She took the boy by the hand and started off toward the hill, leaving the two older couples behind in the mist of the growing dusk. The screeching of the magpies cut across the sky. She tried to match her steps to those of her son.

They called for him several times, from one side to the other. Silvio didn't answer. The girl grabbed the boy by the arm and forced him to walk faster. They would probably find him next to the creek, or what little was left of the creek: a broken stream of chocolate-colored, stinking water, bordered by cattails and yellowing reeds, the slippery and swampy land pockmarked with rabbit burrows and poisonous mushrooms, their stems bent by disease. The girl remembered that when they were children they had caught frogs there, armed with a colander. As the eldest, she'd been the one to go into the water—cold, biting, green—taking care not to splash too much, while Silvio waited, crouched on the bank, keeping quiet with absolute seriousness. Once they'd trapped the frogs, they put them in glass jars filled with water and examined them closely. The frogs almost always ended up suffocating to death, they didn't really know how. The image of a frog floating in the water, its thick legs limp, was one of indescribable sadness. The girl shook off the memory. After all, she thought, there hadn't been frogs there in a long time.

The boy shouted, his throat tight: it was a sharp, child-like call, tinged with uncertainty. There was no answer.

"It's getting dark, *mamá*," he whispered. "Let's go back. *Tito* isn't out here."

The girl stopped to think. They could cross the creek by jumping on some stones without too much risk of getting wet. On the other side, the forest stretched, impenetrable, rustling with pine needles and the fallen bud scales of eucalyptus trees.

Or they could not cross, and continue the search by following the stream until the little dirt road they'd passed that morning upon arriving, the cars still clean and full of food.

"Come," she said. "We're going to cross the creek."

The boy looked behind him fearfully. The purring of a whip-poor-will, the darkness rushing toward him. He swallowed and, grabbing onto the girl, clambered down the slope. They moved forward slowly, holding hands, their shoes sinking in the mud, until they reached the edge of the water. The stream was almost nonexistent. The middle of the creek couldn't have been more than a foot and a half deep. They could hardly make out the stones, flat and muddied, in the shadows. The girl tried to calm the boy. He just had to step really carefully, she told him, put his feet exactly where she put hers. Silvio would be on the other side, she was certain.

The creek stank of stagnant water and rot. The boy whimpered but the girl squeezed his hand and made her way from stone to stone. They went slowly and silently, so as not to lose their concentration. When they stopped talking, the forest filled with sounds: the rustling of reeds, the cry of a small owl, an animal—a rabbit, a rat—running through the rushes, the impossibly far-off rumble of a car.

"Silvio!" yelled the boy, desperate. Then he slipped, and fell in the water.

She didn't have anything else to clean him with so the girl used her own T-shirt to wipe the mud off his legs. His sneakers were drenched but she dried them as best she could and put them back on him. The boy reeked of dirty water. She consoled him for several minutes, humming and cooing. When they stood up, night had fallen completely.

"*Mamá*, shouldn't we go back?"

The boy peered into the darkness of the forest, his pupils dilated.

Locks of hair fell over both sides of his ears, in disarray. His profile blurred into the blackness.

"Don't worry. We're going the right way. I'm sure we'll find Silvio out here."

They called out several more times, feeling their way through the shadows of the trees. Cold and shining silhouettes could still be made out, bathed in moonlight and the glow from some nearby town. The boy moved even closer to the girl and they continued for a few yards, until they couldn't go any farther. They stood still and silent on the cushioned and invisible blanket of leaves.

The question was whether or not they should try to go back. Crossing the creek again was not an option. By now the forest was a *camera obscura*; all identity—of a tree, a thicket, a stone, a puddle—was entirely dissolved. Small insects landed on their exposed calves. All around them were the sounds of leaves and branches rustling swiftly as nocturnal rodents sought a new hiding place, fleeing the barn owls. The reedy, tremulous, drawn-out shriek of a screech owl sounded in the distance, then drew closer with a short, chaotic flapping of wings.

Hoo-hoo-hoo-hoo-hoo.

"It wants us to leave," the boy whispered.

The girl didn't answer. The owl flew overhead for several more minutes until they felt it land somewhere close by.

"Are we lost?" the boy sobbed, clutching at the girl's arm.

"We're fine!" the girl shouted, suddenly on the verge of anger. "Stop whining! You're with your mother, do you hear me? *You're with your mother!* Nothing is going to happen to you! We're not in the middle of the jungle! We're just in some shitty woods by a shitty creek and a bunch of shitty towns and shitty roads! That's all!"

The boy broke into tears and the girl gathered him in her arms. Advancing a few more yards, they shouted as loudly as they could, standing on their tiptoes. At times they stopped to rest and see if someone, in the distance, was calling for them. The only sound was the ominous *hoo-hoo-hoo-hoo* of the screech owl as it glided overhead.

"It wants us to leave," the boy repeated.

"Don't worry. We'll go sooner or later. Are you cold?"

"No, but I'm really tired."

"OK, now listen to me. We're going to lie down to rest a bit and wait until morning. It's OK. This is an adventure, right?"

"Lie down where?"

"Come here," she said.

They went to the foot of a tree and leaned against its trunk. Then the girl crouched down and patted the ground with both hands. It was too hard, small pointy sticks poking up through the ground and scratchy plants, some kind of fern, sprouting wildly here and there. They looked for another tree nearby, feeling their way, stepping slowly, close together with their arms stretched out in the emptiness before them. The screech owl passed overhead again, almost brushing them. The girl cleared the sticks from another patch of earth. The boy stood at her side, controlling his sobs. The girl whispered to him as if he were a baby. *Shhh, easy, child.* Some kind of spider or caterpillar crawled across her hand, but she shook it off and contained her scream. She smoothed the leaves as best she could, breathing heavily. Afterward, she took off her sweatshirt and spread it on the ground, fluffing up the hood near the base of the tree.

"Come," she told him.

She guided the boy to the sweatshirt and showed him where to lie down. Then she stretched out beside him and put her arms around him. The screech owl perched in the tree under which they lay.

The scent of him is sharply sweet and innocent. The boy fell right to sleep, exhausted, and now she feels his deep and uneasy breathing, interrupted at times by the fear that shakes him like a gust. She squeezes his body to give him every molecule of warmth, every single molecule of warmth that can possibly be transmitted by her touch. Curled up at his back, wrapping her woman's legs

around his child's legs, she gently breathes in the smell of his defenseless little
neck, thinking how he was still only half-grown. Despite the sounds, the rustling,
the distant cries, even despite the penetrating call of the screech owl, she can hear
the uneven beat of his pulse, ripping open the night. He's my son, she tells herself,
he's my son.

Two hours or so had passed when the girl heard voices and the barking of
dogs. She opened her eyes and made out beams of light that disappeared
and swung back toward them, the flashing of dreams. The barking came
closer and the owl flew off, hooting and beating its wings. The girl hugged
the boy and remained still a little longer, holding her breath, drinking in
the last moment of freedom, until the boy turned and sat up abruptly,
frightened.

"What's going on, *mamá*? Who's there?"

"Nothing, son," she whispered slowly. "It's OK, they've found us."

They got up and felt the dogs before they could see them—panting,
racing toward the approaching shadows and then returning to touch their
hands with slobbering muzzles. A flashlight shone full in their faces. Her
forearm covering her eyes, the girl pulled the boy in close.

"We're here," she said.

"Oh, thank God."

The figure of Silvio stood out against the darkness; a huge, warm
body standing over them, shouting for a blanket. The boy began to cry
again. The girl was wrapped in a dense and murky confusion. *The sins of the*
past, she remembered. Those words. She felt dizzy, then. Heart racing, still
motionless, she heard the others, their shouts, their noise; the crisscrossing
beams of light, the euphoric barking of the circling dogs, the questions,
the sighs, the smooth touch of the boy's hand, the unmistakable beeping
of the walkie-talkies, the deep voices of the officers giving instructions that
she couldn't quite manage to understand.

Someone came up from behind and took her arm roughly.

"Let's go, girl, get moving. We have to get back. What possessed you to go into the woods with a child this time of night? Bundle him up and follow us. Your family is waiting."

Not letting go of the boy, scarcely giving an answer, she staggered after them, lagging behind. Through the barking of the dogs, she listened for the cry of the owl. She heard nothing.

L

I

N

E

S

IRMA PINEDA is an author, editor, translator, and educator in Juchitán, Oaxaca. She has published seven books of bilingual Isthmus Zapotec-Spanish poetry. She is the only woman to have been president of Mexico's national organization of indigenous-language authors (ELIAC) and is a professor at the National Teachers University.

Guirá dxi naa bacuzaguí

ti batee ni biaxha lu beeu'
ti bianni' dxido' si laa galaa gueela
bele ni ruyaa lú xquendabiaanilu'
biaani' bele dxi'ba' lugialu'
ni rucachi' lade ñeu'
Guié lu

Cada día soy luciérnaga

chispa desprendida de la luna
luz silenciosa en la medianoche
fuego que danza en la memoria
llamarada que cabalga sobre tu cuerpo
para esconder en tus muslos
Sus ojos

T
W
O

Translated by Wendy Call
Zapotec | Spanish | Mexico

Every Day
I'm a Firefly

spark snapped from the moon
silent light at midnight
flame dancing in your memory
blaze that mounts your body
to hide in your muscles
Its eyes

L
I
N
E
S

Pa Guiniu'

Pa guiniu' gubidxa ruuya guendaricaguí
Pa guiniu' guí ruuya xpele beeu
Pa guiniu' yú ricala'dxe' biaani' lulu'
Pa guiniu' nisadó' naa naca guendariati nisa, xizaa ne
     dxiña yaga
Pa naa guinie' sidi, guendaranaxhii, nisadó', gubidxa
lii riniu' guiigu'
       Ne naa raca ti guié

Si Dices

Si dices sol veo el incendio
Si dices fuego creo en la llamarada de la luna
Si dices sangre soy tormenta parada en la tarde
Si dices mar soy sed, angustia y miel
Si digo sal, amor, mar, sol
tú dices río
       Y me convierto en piedra

Translated by Wendy Call
Zapotec | Spanish | Mexico

If You Say

If you say sun I see the flames
If you say fire I believe in the moon's blaze
If you say blood I am the afternoon's raging rain
If you say sea I am thirst, agony, and honey
If I say salt, love, sea, sun
you say river

      And I turn to stone

Pa ma nacaxhiiñilu'
ti guiibaruxale' bindiibi cue'ndaanilu'
ne ti doo naxiña'
ti naxiña' nga die' neza rindani gubidxa
yoo nandxo' ra rialebe
Zacá nga giaapa' xiiñu' ni ca'ru' gale
Ti qui go yaa beeu' laa
Ti guiiba' ruxale ruaa yoo
ti guiibaruxale' rutaagu jneza bi dxaba'
ti guiibaruxale' ne ti doo xiña' zapaca' lii
ti jneza guiale xiiñilu dxi xhanalu'

T
W
O

Si en ti se gesta la vida
una llave cuelga de tu cintura
con un hilo rojo
porque rojo es el color del oriente
recinto sagrado donde nace el creador
Así el hijo que se esconde en ti
no será mordido por la luna
Una llave abre la boca de la casa
una llave cierra el paso del mal viento
una llave y una cinta roja cuidarán de ti
cuando mujer creadora seas

Translated by Wendy Call
Zapotec | Spanish | Mexico

If a life springs within you
hang a key from a red ribbon
at your waist
red is the color of the eastern sky
the creator's sacred birthplace
So the child hidden within you
won't be nipped by the moon
The key opens the front door
the key locks out the evil wind
the key and a red belt will protect you
while you are a creator-woman

L
I
N
E
S

Rarí qui rigaachisi gue'tu' ne ma'
Ñee nalu' rilásicabe ndaani' yu ne riaandacabe
sicasi nusiaandu' ti ziñabanda' lu ti bangu' yu'du' la?
Rarí guendaguti gadxé si laa
rarí nácabe gunaa ni ranaxhii
gunaa ni rusigapa guenda
gunaa nandxo'
gunaa rapa guidapa' ná' guidxilayú
gunaa riete ga' ndaa xha'na' yu
xpixuaana' yoo ba'
ni runi sti' ga' bia'
gunaa ni rapa guendanabani

T
W
O

Aquí los muertos no se entierran nomás y ya
¿crees que se avientan a la entraña de la tierra y se olvidan
como dejar un sombrero en la banca de una iglesia?
Aquí la muerte es otra cosa
aquí es señora amorosa
señora que guarda en su seno el reposo de las almas
señora venerable
señora de los cuatro brazos del mundo
señora de los nueve escalones
gobernanta de la mansión final
dueña de los nueve palmos
señora de la vida eterna

Here the dead don't just go to the grave peacefully
Do you think they're thrown into the earth's bowels
    and forgotten
like a hat left on a church pew?
Here death is something else
here it's a passionate woman
who guards souls' eternal rest in her breast
our blessed lady
our lady of the earth's four directions
our lady of the nine steps
ruler of our final home
queen of the nine handspans
empress of eternal life

L
I
N
E
S

INGER CHRISTENSEN (1935-2009) is known
for her striking innovations in thought, language, and
structure. Her poetry, novels, and essays have been
translated into over thirty languages. During the last
several years of her life Christensen was repeatedly
nominated for the Nobel Prize in Literature.

Når jeg har hørt de tomme rum i huse
fortælle drømme som jeg selv har drømt
og hørt de glemte døre stå og sluse
mine sunkne minder rundt på skrømt

som om der var de store ting at huske
som om det var så vigtigt alt jeg så
som om den vilde blomst de runde buske
var visnet hvis jeg ikke lod dem få

en vokseplads i læ af min bevidsthed
med lys og skygge ligelig fordelt
hvor alt var vundet ved at være mistet
når sproget halvt om halvt var blevet helt

Så har jeg set en jordiskhed i alt
som var mit sind lidt græs der blev fortalt

T
W
O

When I have heard the empty rooms of dwellings
recount the dreams that I myself have dreamt
and heard the doors that I'd forgotten telling
about my sunken memories to a false extent

as if there were big things to recollect
as if each and everything I saw was great
as if the wild flower the rounded hedge
would wither if for them I failed to make

a habitat in the shelter of my mind
with light and shadow equally replete
where all was won by being left behind
when language more or less became complete

Then I have seen an earthliness in all unfold
as if my mind were fine grass being told

L
I
N
E
S

I aften skriver rusens blå Diana
to tusind ord om månelysets vandring
fra glas til glas i helt abstrakt forandring
på et konkret cafébord midt i Lana.

T
W
O
.

Som æblet fra den tabte paradis
står månen over bjergets skrå plantage,
belyser det fortabte pars menage,
et rum for kærlighedens grå forlis.
Hvad kan Diana gøre i sin længsel?
gå på jagt i verdensrummets fængsel,
plukke månen som en bryllupsgave,

spise den så nattehimlen sortner,
dele med sig selv, intil det tordner
af ensomhed i paradisets have.

Translated by Susanna Nied
Danish | Denmark

This evening's gentle high, a blue Diana
writes myriad words about the moonlight's play
on wine glasses, creating abstract changes
on a concrete cafe table here in Lana.

Like the apple in a lost Garden of Eden
the moon floats over sloping hillside groves
throws light on the doomed couple's life together,
a space for the gray shipwreck of love.
What can Diana do in her longing?
Go hunting through the universe, a prison,
pluck down the full moon as a wedding gift

and eat it, so the night sky turns to black;
divide it with herself, until the thunder
of loneliness resounds through Eden's garden.

Translated by Susanna Nied
Danish | Denmark

When I have heard the empty rooms in houses
tell stories from dreams I myself have dreamed
when I have heard the doors that I'd forgotten
bring false notes to my sunken memory stream

as if there were such big things to remember
as if it were so crucial, all I've seen
as if the rounded shrubs and the wild flower
would have withered had they not received

a place of shelter in my consciousness
with light and shadow portioned equally
where everything was won by being lost
when language very nearly was complete

Then in it all I see an earthliness
as if my mind were stories of a patch of grass

This evening writes euphoria's blue Diana,
two thousand words on moonlight's wandering
from glass to glass abstractly transforming
on a concrete café table in central Lana.

Like the apple from the paradise that's vanished
the moon hangs over the hillside's slanting trees,
shining a light on the doomed couple's history,
a space for love's gray wreck of anguish.
What can Diana in her longing envision?
She can go on a hunt in the universe's prison,
pluck the moon as a wedding present,

and eat it so the night sky turns to black,
sharing it with herself until it thunderclaps
out of loneliness in the garden of paradise.

L
I
N
E
S

TAHAR BEN JELLOUN, winner of the Prix Goncourt, has written more than thirty novels, including *The Sacred Night*, *Leaving Tangier*, and the autobiographical novel *L'écrivain public*. Ben Jelloun's prose is at once lyrical, poetic, and rich in fairy tale, imagery, metaphor, and symbolism.

L'écrivain public

T
W
O

Toute ville natale porte en son ventre un peu de cendre. Fès m'a rempli la bouche de terre jaune et de poussière grise. Une suie de bois et de charbon s'est déposée dans mes bronches et a alourdi mes ailes. Comment aimer cette ville qui m'a cloué à terre et a longtemps voilé mon regard? Comment oublier la tyrannie de son amour aveugle, ses silences lourds et prolongés, ses absences tourmentées? Quand je marche dans ses rues, je laisse mes doigts sur la pierre et je traîne mes mains sur les murs jusqu'à les écorcher et en lécher le sang. La muraille résiste même si elle penche un peu; elle ne garde plus la ville mais préserve les souvenirs. Que d'hommes se sont arrêtés au seuil de ces portes immenses, offrant leur corps à la terre et leur âme à l'usure de ce sable rouge!

Mère abusive, fille cloîtrée et infidèle quand même, femme opulente et mangeuse d'enfants, jeune mariée nubile et soumise, corps sillonné par le temps, visage saupoudré de farine, regard déplaçant l'énigme, emporté par le vent, main ouverte posée sur la ville qui dort, épaules larges supportant chacune un cimetière, chevelure longue captive de l'horloge murale, nombril tournant, meule ou moulin à eau, un ventre fatigué, un front ridé, bruit de poutres qui s'étirent, un ruisseau prisonnier dans l'une des murailles, terrasse ouverte, peinte à la chaux vive, femmes assises jambes et bras écartés, ruelles étroites et pierreuses, murs lapidés, délabrés, boue noire, reflet vert, ordures jetées au seuil des portes, épluchures de pastèque et de melon sur tête de veau calcinée, tomates écrasées, nid de mouches dans une vieille babouche, seau d'eau…

Translated by Rita Nezami
French | Morocco

The Public Scribe

Every hometown carries a bit of earth in its belly. Fez filled my mouth with yellow earth and gray dust. Coal and wood soot have settled in my lungs and made my wings heavy. How can I love this city that held me down and clouded my sight for a long time? How can I forget the tyranny of her blind love, her heavy and prolonged silences and her tormented absences? When I walk down her streets, I drag my hand along the stone until my fingers bleed. As time goes by, the walls, which surround the city, lean a little more, but they still hold her memories. Many men have stopped at the city's immense gates, offering their bodies to the land and their souls to the red sand's ravages!

Abusive mother, cloistered yet unfaithful daughter, wealthy child-eating woman, nubile, submissive, newly married, body wrinkled by time, face powdered with flour, a gaze displacing the mystery, carried away by the wind, an open hand placed on the sleeping city, large shoulders each supporting a cemetery, long hair caught on the wall clock, a shapely belly button, grindstone grinding at a water windmill, a tired womb, a wrinkled forehead, sound of beams creaking, a trickle trapped in one of the walls, open rooftops painted with quicklime, women sitting with legs and arms spread apart, narrow, stony, little streets, dilapidated broken walls, black mud, green reflection, garbage thrown at the threshold of doorways, peelings from watermelons and cantaloupes stuck on the burned head of a calf, squished tomatoes, a swarm of flies inside an old *babouche*, some water in a broken plastic bucket, a clump of shaved pubic hair, a donkey carrying crates of grapes, smoke rising from grilled kebabs, a limping beggar, a child running astride a reed, flat streets, lack of air and light, a baker delivering bread, a man pinching a woman in the crowd, a funeral procession, a fat woman walking with a bouquet of flowers in a crystal vase, a wedding procession, including a proud and well-known matchmaker, a ray of sunshine filtering through the palm trees hanging over the market, a panic-stricken mare slipping on the flagstones, a public scribe who has run out of ink, Leila Mourad at the Achabine movie theater, Farid Atrache in a dinner jacket in the film *Matkulchi l'hadd* coming out next week, *Dhohour al Islam* to be released in October. People on rooftops trying to see King Mohamed al Khamis's face in the full moon, sound of a bomb explosion at the Casablanca Central Market, terrified tourists clutching their handbags against their chests, Radio Cairo crackling, there's a lack of water, Fez is closed, curled up in her legends about huge beautiful houses open to the sky; they are cool in the summer and cold in the winter with lemon trees in the courtyards; the houses have heavy, tall, wood-carved doors, kitchens are unventilated and bathrooms are dark, Fez is filled with labyrinths that have seven turns opening on dead ends or on a flooded river carrying the sewers of the entire medina, a mad horse has knocked over vegetable stalls, the horse is going round and round near the dyers, nearly falling into a dye pit, the artisans laugh and the prancing horse neighs through burning nostrils, gets out, crosses the bridge, and falls into the Boukhrareb river, manages to get out, his head bent forward, the current takes along a dead cat in a carton box, the dyers dip rolls of wool into color, they sing and chant, a blind dog brushes past the wall, a child is selling imported cigarettes, a *mokhazni* is playing with an old rifle, a fire alarm goes off at the *Qissaria*, the walls are closing in, the sky is lowering, the earth is trembling, men are running, the face of Fez is full of potholes, it's a silver crater filled with ash, her puffy face has been ravaged by smallpox, it's an ancient face, antique, a work of art displayed by antique dealers, a sculpture work unearthed by some archeologist, face of oblivion, surrounded by thick, high walls, family offspring and social class status are preserved, covered in a red blanket of English wool with cords that are woven with gold and silver yarn, protected from wind and cracks, protected from humidity and envious eyes, Fez has devoured mad love, no knight will come to make the city's legend come true, no woman will throw off her dress and chains at the mosque entrance or at the city gate, no man will be overcome with passion and break the mirrors of past centuries and sing in abandoned meadows, the native city, my native city is advancing toward me and digging up stones and skulls, I am their cemetery, their closed field, where bones are piled up, where no soul makes a stop, where no sky descends; where no ocean flows, I am an orchard surrounded by a wire fence where dogs and donkeys come to copulate, words are dragged across the swollen face of my city, a construction site in full swing, a hideous laughter, a voice without warmth, a hanging tongue and bulging eyes, my native city is in a fictitious land during a make-believe time with made-up characters, veiled silhouettes, where a voice pretends to be mine and thinks it remembers, I do not recognize the voice when it cries out in a serious and even solemn tone because I know it does not concern me anymore. I know the native city has filled my mouth with its earth, with ash and syllables, which I now pass on to the hurrying traveler so that he may disperse some of this earth into the flow of the overflowing *oued*; I can thus leave Fez, forever asleep in the arms of a courtesan with a fallen yet tender and humane spirit; I can finally walk without stones cutting my toes, without a mule crushing me against the wall of a narrow street. So many times have I stumbled on the stones sticking out of the ground, so many times has my head bumped against the low beams and locked doors that lead to a deep mystery. The muddy river smells of excrement, of something suffocating that burns the nostrils; it isn't the twisted head of the horse that the river carries but human body parts, at least that's what I think; I recognize an arm, and a foot with a shoe on, the fast current prevents me from being certain; I leave with a vivid image of a rotting body hitting against the stones. The horse with its gaping mouth must have swallowed the body of the

L
I
N
E
S

unknown dead. I walk along the riverbank, trying to put together the enigma of the body that had been thrown into the mouth of the river, a headless body without a face or a name; it could be anyone's. Oh you worshippers of Allah, has anyone among you lost his body, a head that has gotten separated from its body? Is there an organ in this market of secondhand goods that belongs to the missing body? Nobody has an answer. Hands carrying old dresses, fingers clutching old shoes, an open mouth calling out numbers: fifteen, seventeen, twenty-one; he said twenty-one, do I hear twenty-two? It's going for twenty-three, do I hear more, it can't get any better, twenty-five...the auction market is a paradise for those who wake up before sunrise, it pulsates, it comes and goes, it's life that rises and falls. I watch the vendors: they are impassive; I watch the buyers: they are like statues with worried expressions. I search for the head that would go looking for its body in the river, the heads are clearly visible, so with a stick I poke into the *djellabas* to see what's hidden inside. I give small blows and I sense hard shins, I'm looking for hollow spaces, perhaps this head with the sunken eyes is perched on a stake and the djellaba is empty. Why am I so intrigued by this particular head, and how am I going to inform him that he can find his body, that I saw it alongside the bloated stomach of a dead horse? It's hot in this square, where one can even sell domestic servants at an auction; look at this man who's trying his best to sell torn, moth-eaten curtains; he looks like one who could sell anything and anyone. I start running and can hear my heart drumming; I skip over stones as I run, I spit when I see a dead cat, I hide myself behind a door when I see a horse without a rider. A woman comes out crying, begging for help. She comes out of an obscure street, crying and cursing her fate: Why me? I am only twenty, look at my body, it's young and beautiful. She starts tearing her djellaba and taking off her dress. An old woman throws a sort of blanket over her. How shameful, you shame us all, I don't know you, but if you were my daughter—may God have mercy on me—I would have burned your breasts and stitched up your vagina; but you are a stranger to me, your mother is probably not a good and honorable woman, may God forgive her; come with me and I shall calm you down. No, leave me alone. My husband is crazy. I saw him getting a knife ready. He is going to kill me; I know it, that's my fate. Obscure clouds darken my days, I am only twenty; I am all alone in this world. Oh you good people, help me, come help this poor girl tortured by a madman. Why won't any of you stop to help? You have nothing to fear. Come and see for yourself that he is crazy. Poor girl! May God help her and have mercy on her fallen soul! The young woman turns toward the wall and starts crying with all her might, hitting her head against the stones. A man steps in, a stranger, a passerby, perhaps a foreigner. He doesn't say anything; he just appears from nowhere and guides her out of the street, maybe he's taking her to the hospital. At this moment, the husband charges out of the house, haggard, his shirt torn, with a big knife in his hand; he's looking for his wife and doesn't say a word. A *mokhazni* arrests him; the man doesn't resist, and the street becomes calm again; on the wall remain traces of blood and in one corner lies a woman's babouche.

A new day is beginning. Fez is deeply asleep. The café terraces are empty. Everything is still. I miss the sea. I miss space. The horizon. That's what I miss most in this buried city, a clandestine city that is deprived of the sea, color, and space. I am leaving Fez as one leaves an unfaithful wife or an unworthy mother.

We set out by train for Tangier. We fled like thieves in the night, feeling guilty and really at fault. I know one never truly leaves one's native city. She follows you, fills your sleep with nightmares and premonitions that remind you to return. She lets you die anywhere, yet she wants your body back. Every day, bodies are sent to different corners of the world, to their native cities. The call from the native city is destiny. One cannot escape it.

The train was uncomfortable. There was a fat woman in our compartment who was breastfeeding her child and at the same time eating bread and rancid butter with boiled garlic. We felt like throwing up from the stink. My father lit a cigarette to change the smell in the air.

The woman told him that neither she nor her child could stand the smell of cigarettes. He went out to the corridor, swallowing his urge to vomit. She then prepared another piece of bread and offered it to me. I had to refuse. She became angry, and, with her mouth full, she said: You should not refuse food offered by Allah. I thought to myself: I hope Allah is more merciful and does not mix garlic with rancid butter! I left the compartment to join my father. My mother was holding her head with both hands, trying to fight against the aggravating headache caused by the smell of this terrible food. My brother was asleep as I struggled not to think about hell. They must serve this kind of *tartine* there. My father comforted me by explaining that one does not get to eat in hell. He sounded very certain as he said this. How could he be so sure? In hell, there's time only for burning. So he must have been right. By this time, the woman had stopped eating. She slept, snoring with her mouth open. How to get rid of her? Maybe I should break a windowpane and throw her out? No, that would wake her up. Maybe I should stuff a rag into her mouth and suffocate her? No, one must be realistic. Fez does not forgive those who abandon her. This woman is living proof that the city has a grudge against us. She must have been placed in our compartment by the city's secret agents. In fact, my brother had not been sleeping all this time; he had simply fainted. What a fragile family! I already had a degree in fragility that served as a kind of excuse for me whenever I needed it. My brother must have been jealous of me.

The woman got off at Meknès station. My brother made a mean comment about the smell, something like, "The butcher's refrigerator must have been out of order...luckily she got off." Two thin, pale passengers took her place. They must have been *kif* addicts. I remember seeing a pipe sticking out of one of the men's pockets. They didn't say a word, and very soon they closed their eyes and fell asleep.

My father took out our passports and examined them. Everything looked fine even though we had falsified my date of birth to be able to get into school. Because of my illness, I lost a year. So we changed the real date of my arrival in the world. It's an ambiguity I like, even today. It used to amuse me to hear my classmates announce their birthdays with precision. I always hesitated between 1944 and 1943, on a Thursday morning at ten, at the beginning of a season, maybe during winter. In any case, it could not have been summer as my grandmother had a cold when I was born. What does it matter if it is a year earlier or later? Who cares! Time for me seemed fluid during that period, something that came and went on its own. I liked this ambiguity about my date of birth because it aroused a certain mystery about the beginning of my life.

My brother and I shared the same passport. Looking at the identity picture, I laughed: our prominent cheekbones looked like they were about to crack from laughter. This was my very first photograph, and I was so happy and excited that I couldn't control my giggles. There was nothing funny about it though, but seeing a picture of my face troubled me. What kind of face should one present to the camera? All I knew was that I had to look serious. I hesitated between looking like the serious child that I really was and the carefree kid that I wanted to be. I decided to look like neither. I chose to have a third kind of face that laughs for no reason, that laughs at his own self, or laughs simply because it is required to have some kind of an expression. I wasn't proud of the way it turned out, but it suited me quite well. By this time, I was already posing as the double that I made of myself.

What is this double story? Why have I created my double, for the sake of convenience or out of mischief? What good is it to bring up something that I realized only when I got older? It's better for me to continue talking about what happened later on the train.

The express train always departed on time, but that never guaranteed it would arrive on time. This was because of the Spanish customs checkpoint in Arbaoua. The civil guard was searching for nationalists. Sometimes, they held the entire train hostage, demanding cooperation from the passengers in their search. Zealous people without consciences pointed out fellow passengers in their compartments just so that the train could move on. This happened rarely, though. My father was worried about being searched. The

Spanish had fun humiliating the Moroccans, making them feel as though this country did not fully belong to them. Customs officers' gloved hands went brutally in and out of our pockets. They took away my mother's gold wristwatch. They also arrested one of the two sleeping men sitting across from us. Once the officers left, my father felt relieved; he had been carrying his entire fortune tied around his waist. There wasn't much money, just a little. My mother was upset because of her watch, especially when my father teased her by saying: "It doesn't matter; in any case you can't tell the time!" It wasn't really true though; she taught herself to tell the time using the family wall clock. We arrived in Tangier late in the evening.

The city was illuminated. The sea was a vast blackness lit by the full moon. Lights twinkled from the port at the foot of the hills. The sky seemed to be celebrating, looking almost artificial. Everything glittered in this city. It made me forget the trip's nausea and fatigue. I could already feel this place's affinity for games, lies, and escape. Sensing freedom, I got drunk on deep breaths of the sea. I wanted to be freed from Fez's damp presence, from her stony streets and from the river that cuts through her like a fatality or like a precursor of death.

I was ready for adventure and the kind of liberty that would allow me to be audacious: to look at the sea, touch its foam, run fingers over women's breasts, and store these images in my head to make it through the nights and escape from solitude.

Odor of seaweed, strange and sometimes suffocating, unique smell of the waves from the Mediterranean, huge fish sliced open and cut into pieces on metal counters, bored eyes looking for new adventures, agile hands waving wads of banknotes in the air, hands that sell and buy money, jewelers who are also money changers, marines selling American cigarettes and alcohol from under their djellabas, a rabbi slowly strolling down Siaghine Street, young men boasting about the brothel and about the kindness of Paquita, who just received some exceptional merchandise, all of them less than twenty years old, blonds and redheads imported from the Canary Islands, tourists following a big-bellied guide, prying hands touching foreigners' buttocks, a man slaughtering a cock at the entrance of a mosque, an English woman faints, a Spanish policeman is drinking beer at the Central Café, an American poet is smoking kif while caressing a child sitting on his lap, an old man dressed in white is loudly praising the virtues of Islamic morality, another man is calling for prayers and for boycotting American products, especially Coca-Cola, products which finance the Zionists, a loudspeaker is giving running commentaries on the match of the year between Tangier and Tétouan, a woman in a nightdress and torn panties is getting out of a police jeep swearing on the Spanish policeman's mother's cunt, an itinerant merchant is showing off his mint leaves and green peas from El Faks, an Indian man is lighting incense sticks at the entrance of his store; one street is going up and another coming down, the city square is busy, a big poplar provides shade to a dog cemetery, a hoard of tourists is running behind an amnesiac guide, the low, dry, stone wall where the idlers sit on Boulevard Pasteur, a child is selling shoe laces, Ismail Yassine's picture as an army man is displayed at the Vox, Roxy cinema is showing MGM films only, the novel by Marguerite Gauthier is publicized, *The Violetera* is performed at Goya, a car watchman in a djellaba and bowler hat is walking his hundred steps on the sidewalk and saying: I am an English subject, I am under the British protection, I am a secret ambassador for Her Majesty the Queen, a shoe-shine boy is throwing stones at him, a street is going down, palm trees are bending, windows are closing, linen is fluttering from a balcony, it has arrived tonight as foretold last night by a sailor at the café, it is inevitable because of the full moon, little white waves on the channel announce its arrival, the café owner is nervous, the beach is deserted, we were expecting the wind at the end of the week, it usually arrives as though expelled by the Spanish coasts, doors slam, women from El Fahs clutch their straw hats with one hand and sell cow-milk cheese with the other, the east wind is here, master and lord of the city, it cleans the walls and streets, it sweeps the squares and throws sand into people's eyes, it kills germs and agitates the distraught; the east wind topples everything in its path but also puts things in order, it spreads rumors and its spell holds the city prisoner; the wind is not a legend, its violence provokes a touch of madness, it sweeps the port with huge white waves, its strong gusts are sometimes long and whistling, at other times, they are short and biting, hitting, slapping, overturning everything, tearing the air and making graves shake and even pulling up the dead from their eternal sleep by this invisible and stubborn plague, it whirls endlessly, stopping only for a moment to start its course again. It has raged for ten days, upsetting the smugglers' plans, although some say smugglers use this plague to unload their goods at the foot of the cliffs, we learned that two battered bodies were found on the rocks after the wind calmed down, it's all the better for the smuggling that the coastal police dare not brave it, it's the wind's fault that cartons of American cigarettes are hard to find at the Petit-Socco, and the idlers' low wall remains deserted. We wait for a lull and pray for calm, on the thirteenth day we start cursing the wind again, and when it finally goes away, a strange kind of peace along with doubt lingers in the city as after a long tempest or a shipwreck, people become gentle, they become polite, the wind has subdued them, the moon moves farther away, tables and chairs are again placed on the sidewalks, clandestine lovers kiss in deserted places, windows are reopened and broken panes are replaced, and while some forget, others dread and await the next visit and wonder if it will be as terrible as the one before. How long will we have to tolerate this intruder that destroys everything? Will it come back to spoil the summer by making tourists flee? The east wind is the only character with a sense of humor in this city that sells and buys itself, it is cruel and faithful, it sows doubt and disrupts routine, it comes without warning and rips the sails of the night, leaving little respite for people trying to protect their bodies and their calm.

The scent of cut grass seeps from gardens and cemeteries; when it mixes with the smell of the sea, it makes one feel dizzy. I held my head between my hands, happily going around alone and feeling transported by distant music. I walked through the city with a firm intention of seducing her, possessing her, or at least allowing myself to be embraced by her.

T
W
O

THE FUTURE OF THE FUTURE OF

RA'AD ABDUL QADIR is a pioneer of the Iraqi
"prose poem," the author of five poetry collections, and
a lifelong editor of the literary magazine *Aqlam*. Two of
Qadir's collections were published after his death, after
he suffered a heart attack in 2003. He also left a book-
length manuscript that hasn't yet been published.

نافذة

ظل المطر يسقط أياماً
ظلت تمطر
كانوا ينتظرون أن يقف المطر
لم يقف المطر وظلوا ينتظرون
وظلت تمطر ولم يخرجوا
لم يخرجوا في المطر
لم يقف المطر ولم يخرجوا
لم يفتحوا الباب
لم يقف المطر ولم يفتحوا
وفتحوا النافذة
وتدفق الماء من النافذة
ووقف المطر
وأشرقت الشمس
وطارت الطيور

T
W
O

A Window

It kept raining for days
it kept raining
they were waiting for the rain to stop
the rain did not stop and they kept on waiting
it kept raining and they did not go out
they did not go out in the rain
the rain did not stop and they did not go out
they did not open the door
the rain did not stop and they did not open
they opened the window
and the water came in from the window
and the rain stopped
and the sun shone
and the birds went flying

L
I
N
E
S

نافذتان

يسقط ظله على الشارع
الرجل الواقف في النافذة،
يسقط ظلها على الشارع
المرأة الواقفة في النافذة المقابلة
يسقط المطر على ظل المرأة والرجل
المرأة والرجل يتبادلان قبلة طويلة
تمرق سيارة في الليل
ضوؤها الكاشف يخترق المطر والقبلات

T

W

O

Two Windows

On the street his shadow falls
the man who's standing by the window,
on the street her shadow falls
the woman who's standing by the opposite window,
on their shadows the rain falls
the man and woman share a long kiss,
a car drives by at night, its lights
cut through the rain and kisses.

ثلاث نوافذ

نوافذ منسية لا يطل منها أحد
ثلاث نوافذ لا يكلمها أحد
ثلاث نوافذ مسدلة الستائر
كانت الستائر مرسومة بالطيور
جاء أطفال ورموا النوافذ بالحصى
صرخت النسوة: لقد كسروا زجاج النوافذ
وهرع الرجال بالعصي
وهرب الأطفال مذعورين،
لقد أعادوا الحياة إلى النوافذ الثلاث

T

W

O

Translated by Mona Kareem
Arabic | Iraq

Three Windows

Forgotten windows with no one to look out from them
three windows no one speaks to
three windows with closed curtains
the curtains were printed with birds
the children came and threw stones at the windows
the women yelled: they broke the window glass
the men ran out with the sticks
the children escaped in fear—
they have given the three windows
their life back

PEDRO LEMEBEL was a Chilean essayist, chronicler, novelist, and activist. He was a highly political figure and in *Loco afán*, the collection from which this story is taken, he addresses subjects such as AIDS and the marginalization of transvestites. He died of cancer in 2015.

Berenice
(La resucitada)

T
W
O

Él nunca pensó llamarse Berenice, y menos ponerse ropa de mujer. Solamente huir lejos, escapar de todos esos huasos molestándolo, diciéndole cochinadas. Porque él era un chiquillo raro, feíto, pero con un cuerpo de ninfa que sauceaba entre los cañaverales. Un cuerpo de venus nativa que aunque trataba de ocultarlo entre las ropas enormes que le dejaba su abuelo, siempre había algún peón espiando su baño egipcio en las ciénagas del estero. Apenas asomaba su pubertad, y ya se le notaba demasiado su vaivén colibrí en el mimbre de esclava nubia perdida entre las pataguas. Por detrás era una verdadera chiquilla, una tentación para tanto gañán temporero que no veía mujer hacía meses. Hileras de inquilinos que pasaban en la tarde gritándole: Mijito tome esta frutita. Mijito cómase esto, cabrito vamos p'a los yuyos. Por eso al cumplir los dieciocho años se fue, cansado que lo jodieran tanto. Se juntó con un grupo de mujeres que iban a la corta de uva y partió entre ellas riéndose y haciendo chistes. Se despidió de su tía y del abuelo, que eran su única familia, y dijo que se iba con ellas porque no lo molestaban, que cortar uva no era difícil, y con lo que ganara se iba a comprar un pasaje a Santiago.

Así, desapareció de esos tierrales, de ese paisaje alborotado por las chiquillas, las cabras vecinas, sus amigas que lo convencieron que se fuera con ellas más allá de los cerros, donde el campo azulado de viñas congregaba a las temporeras de la zona. Todas esas mujeres de brazos…

Berenice
(Risen from the Dead)

It had never occurred to him to call himself Berenice, still less to put on
women's clothes. He just dreamed of going somewhere far away from
there, to escape all those hicks bothering him with their smutty remarks.
Because he was an odd little boy, rather ugly, but with the body of a willowy
nymph of the canefields. With the body of a native Venus and, however
hard he tried to conceal this beneath the baggy clothes his grandfather
gave him, there was always some farmhand watching him bathing in the
muddy waters of the stream. Almost as soon as he reached puberty, his
humming-bird flutterings, like those of some Nubian slave lost among
the reeds, were all too obvious. From behind, he looked like a young girl,
a real temptation to any migrant worker who had not seen a woman in
months. To the lines of farmers who passed by in the evenings, shouting:
Have I got a lovely juicy fruit for you, sweetheart. Have a bite of this, kid,
come into the bushes with me. That is why, as soon as he turned eighteen,
he escaped, tired of being pestered. He joined a group of women off to the
grape harvest and left, laughing and making jokes. He said goodbye to
his aunt and his grandfather, who were his only relatives, and explained
that he was going with the women because they didn't bother him, that
harvesting grapes wasn't such hard work, and with what he earned, he
could buy a ticket to Santiago.

So he disappeared from that dustbowl, from that landscape, urged on by his friends, the local girls, who persuaded him to go with them beyond the hills, to the blue fields of vines that drew all the female seasonal workers. All those women with strong arms, ladies with hands grown hard from working the land and from other farming tasks. They worked from sunrise to sunset, scattered along the rows of vines. Ants wearing straw hats, holding out against the drowsiness that would hit them at three in the afternoon. When the yellow planet would plunge its fiery sword into their heads. When there wasn't even a scrap of shade to give them some respite from their scorching work of harvesting the grapes from the low vines. When the sun is the foreman, flaying their skins with his burning whip. Then the only thing that dulls fatigue is a little hope. Perhaps some new jeans for Luchín, whose only other pair is in tatters. Perhaps that colorful cloth from the village shop to brighten up the table. Or, if there's enough money, a blouse, a flowery skirt, some cheap rouge, some moisturizer to rub on sunburned cheekbones. And lots, lots more, so many possibilities, so many miracles in the form of new curtains or else dresses for their little girls. All those daydreams depending on so few pesos, the sum of all the many baskets they will never manage to fill in just one day. The young girls do it at a run, rushing to fill up the baskets and earn enough money to buy a secondhand American parka and some sneakers, made by Bata, but just as good as Adidas.

And among those young women as fresh as green shoots, almost indistinguishable among the coquettish gestures, the boy laughs contentedly, splashing his companions with water, leavening the hard work with his effeminate gestures, telling the women not to bend like that. No, love, you'll end up looking like a camel. Watch me. Like this, without hunching, keeping your spine absolutely straight. You bend from the knees, as if you were picking up a flower fallen on the road. Then the women would do as he said, killing themselves laughing, amidst applause, shouts, and blown kisses, filling the afternoon like sweet birdsong.

It was during that summer of febrile grapes and women's sweat that he acquired the name Berenice. It was quite unplanned, for how was he to know that the 35-degree heat of that February sun frying their brains would claim a victim? A death among the women who would often faint in the fields, and then, having drunk some water and rested for a while, return to the exhausting task of picking the grapes. But one of them, no more than a kid, really, with a weak heart, did not come around again. And although they tried to revive her by splashing her with water and fanning her with vine leaves, her breathing only grew more and more labored. She lay dead among the bunches of grapes, her dark, oval face staring up at the sun. Almost proud to die like that, cushioned by the succulent softness of that mattress of vines. Then her colleagues stopped working and stood dumbstruck for a moment, unable to take in what had happened. And then people rushed forward and shouted and asked who she was, if anyone knew her, who would tell her family. What would the bosses say, sitting up there in their office drinking mineral water. It was those lousy exploiters who were responsible for her death. And they all marched off, furious, brandishing their pruning shears. No, not you, they said to the boy, you're not a woman. You stay here and look after the dead girl and stop the ants from eating her. And they left him keeping tremulous watch over the body. Because he had never watched over a body before. Apart from this one, and she was really pretty when you studied her properly. She looks like a virgin, he said to himself, closing her eyes. But even a virgin must have a name, some means of identification. And he started feeling around in the pockets of her pinafore until he found a battered, stained identity card. And Berenice was born at that very moment, when he looked at the photo and read the name. He saw himself reflected in that identity as if in a mirror. And with a little imagination, perhaps by plucking his eyebrows... He could do it, why not? And he didn't think twice, re-baptizing himself with the identity of the dead girl, whom he thanked with a kiss on her still-warm forehead. Then it was just a matter of disappearing, and traveling and traveling until he found himself beneath the smoky skies of the capital. He made himself look more like the photo on the identity card by letting his hair grow long, Indian-fashion; a little makeup, some filling for his bust, and a soft voice. Thus, like a carnation grafted onto a rose, he set forth full of the pirated innocence of his new identity, as Berenice, risen from the dead.

Time in the city is a piece of cloth that soon wears thin, especially for an out-of-towner who makes it pass even faster in the somersaults he must perform in order to survive. The mornings, then, are spent staring at the famous faces in the magazines on the newspaper stands, reading headlines in which he will never appear. But this was not the case with Berenice, who leaped to fame as a crazed kidnapper, and took up the whole of the front page in all the papers. Filling the TV screens, displaying the eunuch motherliness of the Virgin Mary or the Mother of the Year, like a shell or a basin surrounding the baby she had stolen from the wealthy house where she was working as a nanny—the only decent job she could find in the city, after years and years working her butt off on the streets with the other transvestites. Because she didn't want to end her life like those other faggots-by-birth. She never forgot the South, or the cloudy skies, like the tail of a gray fox entangling itself in her dreams. That's why she hated all the makeup, all the paint her colleagues used, all the high heels and wigs and gaudy clothes they vainly tried to press on her. They couldn't take the peasant girl out of her, she wouldn't even wear earrings or false eyelashes to brighten up her eyes grown dry amidst all the concrete. Not even a bit of eye shadow or rouge to liven up her scrubbed-clean face, like that of an early-rising nun. That's why you don't get the best clients, just the plain-clothes cops and the Mapuche Indians who mistake you for a maid, the other transvestites told her. And that, it seemed, would be her future. And she didn't mind being mistaken for a hard-working Indian, the sort you just can't find anymore, the sort who never demands any holidays or wants to have their social security contributions paid. The sort who can clean

T
W
O

like nobody's business, who doesn't wear miniskirts or wiggle their ass at the boss. The kind of healthy Indian who will make do with very little, just a pittance for a salary, a tiny room, and some food. Just that and all the time in the world to drool over the mistress's baby whom Berenice so adored. The little baby with golden curls whom she stole in a moment of high emotion when the child called her "Mama." She simply couldn't take it, she could find no memory in which to store that little word, and she felt tenderness bubbling up in her belly, as if the word filled her with buds that burst into roses out of every pore. That word scrambled her brain, already so scrambled by all that changing of sex. That "Mama" completely undermined her little bird-heart, and she didn't think twice, she ran off with the baby as if she were stealing a doll from an expensive store. Out of pure love, because the baby had happened to address the wrong breast as "Mama," and that was a song no one had ever sung to her before. Because, down there in the South, her aunt and her grandfather had never told her where she had come from. All she remembered from the past were the words "bastard" and "fairy" that the other children had shouted after her. That is why she took some clothes, some savings and left with the little boy, telling him: We're going to the zoo zoo zoo, how about you you you, you can come too too too, we're going to the zoo zoo zoo. She said they would buy candy, balloons, toys, and anything else he could possibly want. That they were going to have a great time on the bus heading south, far from Santiago, far from radios broadcasting news of the kidnapping. Far from the police studying her fingerprints and discovering that Berenice was a man. Far from the child's weeping parents, who begged the homosexual kidnapper not to harm him. The whole of Chile thinking the worst, imagining the child being subjected to the most terrible sexual atrocities at the hands of that degenerate. The police looking for her, sending faxes all over the country, bearing the innocent, expressionless face of an absent Berenice. Or, rather, the photo of an identity buried six feet under in the South, all those years ago. The dead face of the original Berenice, photocopied beneath the earth,

L
I
N
E
S

pursued beyond that final disappearance by her transvestite double. Perhaps rescued from her anonymous grave, exhumed in a masculine version that mocked the official document. Revived or perhaps reinvented in the gutter press as an urban adventure rather than as a mad longing for motherhood.

Thus, that face from the South unsettled the everyday life of the nation and rattled polite society. For hours and hours they were bombarded by the news of the kidnapping being trumpeted by the newscasts. As for Berenice, now doubly disguised as a mother, she was playing with her little boy in a square in a provincial town. Both of them were laughing and running about, chasing each other, screaming gleefully in the excitement of "Ready or not, here I come," laden with pinwheels and paper birds, sticky with sugary clouds of rosy sentiment. They stuffed themselves with tidbits, meringues, and dragées, spending all their money on fripperies that made them happy. She bought him a cowboy hat, a Batman cape, an Ultraman sword, and a big toy rabbit which served as a pillow when the little boy fell asleep, exhausted. When evening came, they curled up together on a bench, fugitives, unable to go to a hotel or seek shelter in the church. Which is why, right there, nestled together on that bench blooming with toys, she sang him "Rockabye baby on the tree top," whispering it hoarsely, in her faggot-cum-mother's voice. Doting as a mother hen, she showered him with kisses, lulling him to sleep with "When you wake, you shall have all the pretty little horses." And as if by magic, the little park formed a bell of silence around them, and let them go on dreaming the same game together. Tired out, they both lay down, and darkness tiptoed in, and, in the great empty square, the country night covered them with its blue veil.

That is how the police found them, curled up together in the night of lonely love. When the story had barely begun, when she had only just closed her eyes, the curtain fell for Berenice, caught in the shock of capture. Yet she seemed unsurprised, as if she had woken up knowing that the party was over. Frozen in the photo in the newspaper, she handed back the child as if she were handing back a borrowed toy. She didn't make a fuss, but emptied her pockets of sweets, wrapped the child in his Batman cape and gave him his Ultraman sword and the cowboy hat. She did not even shed a tear, just said goodbye to him gently, undramatically. The only thing she kept back was the toy rabbit, taking with her the smell of the little boy's sleep on the soft, wet fur.

L
I
N
E
S

Born in Jerusalem in 1978, **NAJWAN DARWISH**
is an acclaimed Palestinian poet who writes in Arabic.
His work has been translated into over twenty
languages, and his 2014 book *Nothing More to Lose*
was listed as one of NPR's best books of the year.

سمعته يغنّي

هذه القصيدة مكتوبة إلى إنسان تحطمت بلاده
ما بقي في يده مَنَحني إياه
وكما في الحكمة القديمة «لا يملك شيئاً ولا شيء يملكه»
من قاع الحطام سمعته يغنّي:
«يا مارق ع الطواحين والميّة مقطوعة»
وكانت المياه والكهرباء والآمال
كلّها مقطوعة.

T
W
O

I Heard Him Singing

This poem is written for a man
whose country was destroyed
and who gave me all he had left
· in his hands, as in the proverb
"Possess nothing, and nothing possesses you."
From the depth of destruction, he sang:
"You, passing by the mills when the water's been cut off."

Water, electricity, hope:
they were all cut off.

حجر فى الريح

قلتُ هؤلاء لا يعرفون أهلي
لا يعرفون «عمر» ولا «صلاح الدين»
لا يعرفون بائعات العنب يسلن كالماء من أرياف القدس
لا يعرفون فتية الحيّ مضوا إلى الشهادة كأنما إلى سهرة أصدقاء
لا يعرفون جميلات العيون من وراء الألثمة
لا يعرفون المقاليع في أيديهن المعطرة
لا يعرفون كيف فتّتنا حجر الحب وألقيناه في الريح
لا يعرفون...
لا يعرفون...

T
W
O

A Stone in the Wind

I said, Those people don't know my family.
They don't know Omar or Saladin.
They don't know the women selling grapes and flowing
from the countryside around Jerusalem.
They don't know the neighborhood boys who walked
serenely into martyrdom
as if spending an evening with friends.
They don't know the beauty of the women's eyes
behind the *kaffiyehs*,
the slingshots in those perfumed hands.
They don't know how we broke the stone of love
and threw its pieces to the wind.
They don't know.
They just don't know.

L
I
N
E
S

لستَ شاعراً في غرناطة

عندما وجدتُ نفسي منسياً في شوارعك
عرفتُ أنني في مدينتي
قلتُ لنفسي ليس المرء نبياً في مدينته ولستَ شاعراً في غرناطة
ومثل ولدٍ عليّه أن يُكافح عشرين سنة في غرفته ليحظى بالوقوف عند
أوطأ عتبات الشعر
عليّ أن أكافح طويلاً في حجراتك دون أن تعرفيني.
أنت مثل بلادي قلّما رأتني
عوّدَتني على النسيان وبه كانت تهدهد سريري
حتى أصبح النسيان بيتي.

سعادتي اليوم أن أنسى
مثل شجرة رمّانٍ نسيها النسيمُ
في واحدةٍ مِن حدائقك.

T
W
O

Translated by Kareem James Abu-Zeid
Arabic | Palestine

You Are Not a Poet in Granada

When I found myself forgotten on your streets,
I knew I was in my city.
I told myself that man
is not a prophet in his city
and that you
are not a poet in Granada.
Like a boy struggling for twenty years
alone in his room
to gain a foothold at the lowest rungs of verse,
I must struggle in your rooms
without your knowing me.
You are like my country—seldom has it seen me,
yet it acquainted me with oblivion
and rocked my bed with it
until oblivion became my home.

My joy, today, is to be forgotten
as the wind forgets a pomegranate tree
in one of your gardens.

بلد يسمّى الأغنية

عشتُ في بلدٍ يسمّى الأغنية
مغنيات بلا عدد منحنني الجنسية
ملحّنون من جميع الأصقاع
ألّفوا لي مدناً بصباحاتٍ وأمسيات
وكنتُ أتنقّل في بلدي
مثلما يتنقّل إنسانٌ في جميع الأرض.

بلدي الأغنية
وما إن تتوقف حتى أعود لاجئاً.

Translated by Kareem James Abu-Zeid
Arabic | Palestine

A Country Called Song

I lived in a country called Song:
Countless singing women made me
a citizen,
and musicians from the four corners
composed cities for me with mornings and nights,
and I roamed through my country
as a man roams through the world.

My country is a song,
and as soon as it ends, I go back
to being a refugee.

أندلسيون

لا أعرف كيف أُسمّي هذا الأسى
الذي يَغلي كَمِرجلٍ في النفس حتّى ليوشك أن يخنق صاحبه،
يتجدّد في «عيد جميع القدّيسين»...
أندلسيون خذلتهم ملائكةٌ وأشجار وشموس
لم يصدّقوا دماءهم في المذبحة
ولم يصدّقوا تشرّدهم في الأرض
كما لا أُصدّق رجوعي الناقص هذا
مثل شبح قتيل يعود إلى الساحة التي أُعدِم فيها
فيجدها خَالية
إلا من الأغنيات.

Translated by Kareem James Abu-Zeid
Arabic | Palestine

Andalusians

I don't know what to call this grief
that seethes like a cauldron within the self
until it's almost suffocating,
this grief that's always renewed
on All Saints' Day.
The Andalusians, forsaken by angels, trees, and suns,
believed neither their blood in the slaughter
nor their vagrancy on the earth,
just as I do not believe
this incomplete return of mine,
like a ghost coming back
to the scene of its execution
to find it empty of everything—
everything
but songs.

L
I
N
E
S

Engaging the
New Knowledge

MADHU H. KAZA

For most of my school years beginning in the second grade I studied French. By the time I reached college, I was reading novels and writing papers in the language, error-ridden though they were. A decade after I stopped studying it, I used French for the first time outside of the classroom, making a trip to Paris when I was nearly thirty years old. I missed quite a lot of the Parisian slang, but on a research trip years later to Chamonix in southwest France I found that I was able to navigate interviews and archives comfortably. I'm not fluent, but the grammar is imprinted in me after all those years of drills. Still, I've used French so little in my life. I'm not sure—as the schoolgirl might ask—what it's for.

I studied Spanish formally for three weeks in Mexico the summer before I began a graduate program in comparative literature. All those years spent in submission to the rules of French, it turned out, did serve a purpose: learning Spanish was easy. I make many mistakes, but given the three weeks versus ten years of study, I am much more at ease speaking and reading Spanish than French. Italian, I studied for one semester, sitting in on an intensive beginner's class in order to pass a proficiency exam. I enjoyed speaking Italian, its drawn-out vowels in particular. I only learned the basics, enough to talk to a bus driver in Rome or read a magazine. Two summers ago I spent a few weeks working on Portuguese on the Duolingo App. I had just finished writing an essay about Clarice Lispector and I wanted more intimacy with her work than reading her in English (and in

Spanish translation) allowed. After I breezed through the exercises on my subway commute for two weeks, the app told me that I was 40 percent fluent in Brazilian Portuguese, but I understood that I was simply 40 percent fluent in Duolingo. I can't hear Portuguese at all. In college I had also studied Hindi for two semesters, which means I can read and write the language, but my vocabulary is so limited I mostly tell people, "Hindi nahi aati"—I don't know Hindi. I got halfway through a semester of Danish, until I got kicked out of the class because auditors were not allowed. I continued for a few months to study it on my own.

I enjoy languages. I'm good at learning them and don't fret as much as I might about my lack of mastery. I can imagine translating from French or Spanish and, with greater effort, Italian. Recently an acquaintance and colleague approached me about collaborating on a translation of essays by Inger Christensen. Though neither of us is proficient in Danish, my answer was a hopeful and enthusiastic, yes. The language that I cannot imagine translating from is Telugu. Though English is the language of my greatest fluency, Telugu is my first language. In the last decade, I have translated contemporary Telugu fiction into English, and yet it remains improbable to think of myself as a translator from this language. I have never been able to articulate the difficulties of this work, tied as they are to my status as an immigrant and to problems of cultural difference.

Literary translation requires great skill and attention, of course. I don't mean to sound cavalier about the real challenges of any translation task and don't claim that translating from European languages is easy. When I say I can imagine translating from French and Spanish or Italian or even Danish, I'm not suggesting that I would be a great translator from any of these languages. I have, in fact, translated some poetry from Spanish, which I struggled with for all the usual reasons that translating poetry is difficult. I mean, instead, to emphasize the word "imagine." Translating from world-dominant languages is imaginable, apart from the issue of one's skill, precisely because of their dominance and circulation in the world.

So I want to talk about something other than individual skill. Questions of skill, considerations of all the technical fault lines of translation, take up so much space in discussions of literary translation in the U.S. that they obscure other kinds of problems we might also engage. Translation issues that are less often named, for instance, include questions of literary values and their connection to culture and power. In thinking about my own experience of translating from Telugu, the problem of skill gives way to questions of access (how does one acquire and strengthen skills) and cultural difference (what gets recognized as skill in writing in English, and in Telugu?), and I think what's at stake is not only a question of diversity or inclusion, but the kind of literary cultures we want to participate in and build.

I translate because I am an immigrant. I write and think and dream in a language distant from my origins, but a language that has become a home. I was brought to the U.S. by my parents when I was five years old. They had immigrated a few years earlier and sent for me when they were sufficiently settled. It's not an unusual immigration story. On my fifth birthday, I left my home, my school, friends, neighbors, extended family, my language, a whole world and way of life as well as my grandmother and grandfather who had parented me up until then. I lost a life and traveled toward a new one. If translation is the "afterlife" of a text as Walter Benjamin first put it, I think of all of my life in the U.S. and in English as the afterlife of a child who was raised in a small town in coastal Andhra Pradesh, India. I am living out a translated life. Like many child immigrants I wonder about the person I would have become if I had not left home, the girl whom I had abandoned.

The difficulties with translation from Telugu began, then, with a split in my self. Or to put that statement in reverse: the very knot of identity for me is connected to problems of translation, of what can and cannot be transmitted across borders. If assimilation were easy, if one life and one identity could be converted smoothly into another, I would not need to translate. But the different parts of my identity sit in jagged, disproportionate relation inside me, and Telugu and English are two languages that almost never meet in my current North American life. Virtually no Telugu literature in translation has been published in the U.S. Because Telugu is a vernacular rather than national language, English translations circulate primarily on the Indian subcontinent itself.

I didn't come to translation from a love of a particular Telugu writer or a general interest in Telugu literature. I wanted very badly as a young adult to be returned to something that had been disappeared from my life, to find a way to carry the language I had left behind with me. I felt the desire for the language of my infancy, what Dante understood as the emotional call of "the language of the cradle." Because it includes the intimacy created with first words, it is a deeply felt but difficult yearning for me to describe, and it's far from literary. When I was growing up in the American Midwest in the 1980s it seemed not only as if the language had been voided in me, but also as if the language itself was obscure and dying in the world. It was spoken within the Telugu community in the U.S., but most people outside that community didn't even know that the language existed. To not have the language recognized meant I had to bury that essential, original part of my identity. I didn't think I could ever get close to the language again. Once my Telugu speaking relatives died, I imagined it would die out in me as well.

There was a book in my parents' house called *The History of the Kammas*, which is the caste I belong to. Although the cover was titled in English, the book itself was written in Telugu. I recall looking through the book many times, lamenting that I would never be able to crack open knowledge of where I came from because I could not read the script. I think it was that book that first made me want to try to learn to read Telugu. My first attempt at study was the summer after I graduated from high school. I spent a month at my aunt's house in India, and she arranged to have her friend, a teacher, give me Telugu lessons one hour a day at 7:00 a.m. There was no pedagogy for teaching Telugu to English speakers, and his antiquated schoolteacher style meant that I mostly repeated syllables and words without comprehending what I was saying. Nothing came of it.

In college at the University of Michigan I perused books in the graduate library on the history of Andhra Pradesh and Telugu. The library held books written in Telugu, but I couldn't read them. There were a significant number of students from Telugu speaking families at Michigan and so, in my second year of college I spoke to the head of the South Asian Studies program asking what it might take to get Telugu language classes started at the university. At that time the only university offering courses in Telugu in the U.S. was the University of Wisconsin in Madison, where Telugu scholar V. Narayana Rao taught. I was told that I would need to raise at least a million dollars for the university to set up an endowed chair or I'd need to raise thirty thousand dollars for a contingent instructor for a year. I decided to try to raise thirty thousand dollars from the Telugu community of southeastern Michigan. I drew up a list of people who said they would be interested in taking a class if it were offered and spent a few months on a fundraising campaign. But I was an unconvincing nineteen year old, and the people with the deepest pockets in the community were professionals who wanted their own children to get professional degrees. They were unsentimental about their own language and saw no prospects or future in it. I abandoned my naïve campaign and made a plan to spend a summer learning to read and write Telugu in Wisconsin. It was a revelation that summer to move from orality to literacy as an adult. I discovered that I knew how to make statements or ask questions in Telugu but I didn't always know the component words in a speech act. I was far from being skilled enough in the language to translate, but I had gained a rudimentary literacy. This, I realized, allowed me to grow out of a childlike relation to the language; to be able to navigate traffic signs or read a newspaper strengthened my sense of belonging to a contemporary culture. What opened up was the possibility of engaging the language in its greater complexities, of moving from an intimate and emotional personal connection to the language to the consideration of a wider cultural discourse through the writing of others.

The following year I spent two months in India and during this time I set up Telugu lessons with a retired professor in Hyderabad. Now that I could read, I was aware of how stunted my vocabulary was and I wanted to build greater fluency in the language. I had to arrange for a car and driver to take me from one end of Hyderabad to his home in Secunderabad, an hour's drive. The professor was a warm and learned man, but he was clearly dismayed by my lack of sophistication in the language. My lexicon was limited to the diction of day-to-day life and I read very slowly. On more than one occasion, when I arrived at his house his wife informed me that he was out on an errand or having coffee with his friends. She would bring me a cool drink and fruit and urge me to wait until he returned. In the Indian manner she told me that he'd be back any minute, which meant eventually. On those occasions, I'd wait for a little while to be polite and then leave. In those two months, I learned a few dozen new words and my reading level remained unchanged. All through these years, I attended a number of Telugu literary events and conferences in the U.S. organized by local Telugu community organizations. I was, without exception, the only young person at these events. I understood very little of what I heard because the texts being discussed were written in a formal, literary Telugu, whereas I only understood the demotic, and because I didn't know the literary history and culture. While the elders were vaguely pleased that I was interested in Telugu literature, they didn't want to interrupt their conversations to break the text or the conversation down to my level. I was still much too slow to gain entry into these groups and so, again learned very little. The turning point for me came in 2005, thirteen years after I first attempted to study Telugu, when Sitaram Ari, a translator and friend of my parents, asked me to collaborate on translating a book of contemporary Telugu short stories. The collaboration was the bridge I needed.

I relate this sad history because I want to be clear that for many years my attempts to engage the language were charged with futility, a constant, chronic feeling of failure. This failure, I recognize only now, was not about my potential talent for or sensitivity to the language, nor was it about my abilities as a writer. I simply didn't have a way. Literary translation is always the result of enormous labor; that labor includes years of study and reading that precedes any particular translation project. And that labor requires either preexisting privilege and knowledge or access to resources and an infrastructure to support the study of foreign languages. With French, Spanish, or any number of other languages I would certainly have struggled to gain fluency, but I understood that there were paths: the college courses, the study abroad, the intensive reading, graduate school, and so on. My lack of access to Telugu was structural, not an accident of individual circumstances; nor was it an indicator of actual Telugu literary production. Though few people in the U.S. have heard of it, Telugu is not obscure. It is a major language, with over eighty million speakers worldwide, one of the top fifteen languages spoken in the world. And the lack of translation from Telugu is not due to a lack of a written culture. Telugu has a longstanding literary tradition which includes a Sanskritized classical language and a vibrant modern literary culture in the contemporary demotic. But it's far easier in the U.S. to find literature translated from Dutch or Italian or Hungarian, for example, than from Telugu (or other South Asian languages for that matter). Given that Telugu is more widely spoken than Dutch, Italian, or Hungarian, and given its long and active literary tradition, what accounts for the disproportionate difficulty of accessing Telugu? What accounts for the absence of Telugu literature in English translation outside of India? The answers are complex, but I think they are neither strictly aesthetic nor geographical, but about how aesthetics carry a politics and history.

When I began translating from Telugu I ran into a major difficulty: a clash of literary cultures. I could readily see that much of the work that I had begun to read would not be easy to get published in the U.S. Telugu literature is quite different in style and sensibility from contemporary American writing. I could imagine editors in the U.S. receiving Telugu writing in translation saying (and they did), "It's just not a good fit for us." This phrase is one that many of us have heard in our lives in contexts where decisions around inclusion are being weighed, for instance in the arenas of publishing and employment. It's a phrase that's been directed at me and one I've heard from the other side as a member of hiring and academic search committees. It's not difficult to recognize this euphemistic phrase as a cover for unexamined bias. What does it mean? What is the phrase doing as a speech act other than closing the door with a feigned politeness and no explanation? I'm not arguing here that people are owed detailed explanations of rejection. Rather, I'm interested in how such a phrase short-circuits the possibility of self-reflection among cultural gatekeepers. It would be easy to simply call people or institutions out as biased. But I'm looking for a way to think past the impasse of saying that something or someone is not a good fit. One way to do this is to examine more closely what we find ill fitting, not only by articulating what a work of art is doing, and the values that launch the work, but also naming our own aesthetic values and situating them in the context of a particular time and place.

Translation is an obvious site to think through difference because there's no way around problems of incompatibility whether it's the incompatibility of words and idioms in different languages or differences in literary traditions and cultural values. What translation opens us up to is not only the wider world of which we are a small part, but also the possibility of seeing our own culture more clearly and considering how the language and literatures of others might expand and alter our own traditions. In *This Little Art*, Kate Briggs argues that translation might be viewed not as the result of a translator's expertise in transmitting something already known and understood from one language to another, but as "productive of *new* knowledge." She writes that it leads us to an "as yet un-acquired, un-grounded, knowledge of the world—of experiences and stories, ideas and things, people and places, tastes and smells, rhythms and sounds."

I think the new knowledge that extends to other places, things, ideas, creates an opportunity to reencounter what we already know—the people, places, rhythms, ideas of our own culture—and makes space for strands of thought not yet present or possible.

Ultimately, I think it's limiting to maintain an assimilationist, domesticizing stance that translation shows us that other people are just like us. If we need others to be just like us, then our idea of the human is a problem. It's important not simply to identify with others but to create bridges across points of disidentification. Translation also shows us that people are different—they think and write and organize their lives differently than we do. What emerges from this difference is the opportunity to see our own lives in new ways and to energize our literary culture. Exposure to other literatures creates unexpected possibilities for Anglophone writing. One question, though, is what gets through? How much difference and what kinds of differences do we allow?

As in other world literatures, the figure of the writer in Telugu culture, unlike in the U.S., is connected with the role of the intellectual. The writer is recognized as a thinker of public and moral standing and very likely a partisan. Telugu fiction doesn't eschew ideology. Writers identify as Dalit, Marxist, feminist practitioners. Individual sensibilities certainly come through, but writing is directly connected to social and political worlds. Much of contemporary Telugu fiction arises from a social realist aesthetic. It doesn't lean toward a Western or global reader; it's a literature for its people. When I first started reading Telugu, I didn't immediately love the stories I was translating. They were feminist stories of women coming to an awakening in a deeply misogynist society, but I found the stories somewhat didactic, overly sociological. I didn't think they were all that good. But I knew that I would have to think past this first judgment. I couldn't dismiss the quality of the work without further interrogation, nor could I assume my reaction was an innocent matter of taste. To reject the work outright because it didn't meet my expectations of style would be reenacting a colonial violence. In 1835, Lord Macauley delivered his famous Minute on Indian Education in which he claimed that "a single shelf of a good European library was worth the whole native literature of India and Arabia." This assessment was explicit justification for a colonial project of English education that intended to create "a class of persons, Indian in blood and color, but English in taste, in opinions, in morals, and in intellect." Such a class was formed to help govern the colony. In a contemporary context, the rejection of a vernacular literature which doesn't adhere to American aesthetics or to a global style, can reinforce neo-imperialism through the market-driven demand for more easily translatable and easily consumable global fiction.

We could perhaps embrace work that doesn't fit with our own aesthetic expectations on anthropological grounds. In the spirit of inclusion we might acknowledge, for instance, that contemporary Telugu fiction reflects its culture and read it primarily for cultural information. This anthropological approach presents its own problems. At best it is patronizing, at worst another form of cultural violence. The Iraqi born writer and translator Sinan Antoon has written about the neocolonial approaches to Arabic literature after the 9/11 terrorist attacks, in which it is read and translated not as literature, but for its "forensic interest" which treats it as "anthropology or ethnology or getting into the Arab mind." Here translation serves a suspect tactical project of engaging the other. Even in a less-charged context, for example the case of Telugu, it is a form of cultural condescension to disregard the fact that the texts of the other culture are constructed as *literature*, that they are made with aesthetic ideas in mind. I think it's imperative to greet other literatures with questions that are beyond sociological, by engaging the literary values that inspire the work.

If we recognize, for instance, that Telugu literature is grounded in different literary values than American fiction, we might note that in Telugu, literature is more directly valued for its role in social change. Telugu values telling as much as showing. Such differences, though, lead us back toward something else: a consideration of our own values.

American writers tend to think of themselves as not ideologically marked. But like white privilege or male privilege that idea signals a kind of blindness. (It's not surprising that the Telugu writers I've met are mostly interested in African-American writing in the U.S.) The dominant American style of fiction is one in which the writer takes care not to take too clear of a moral stance. It is considered a defect if a work contains sociological elements. The writer should focus on showing and not telling, image not exposition. American writing is anti-intellectual. But we know that these attitudes are themselves a result of cold-war ideology. The CIA was directly involved in channeling artists and writers toward nonpolitical, abstract work compatible with American individualism and capitalism. The CIA funding of important institutions such as the *Paris Review* and the Iowa Writers Program is well documented.

I'm not arguing that we need to abandon our aesthetic values and ideals. Rather, I'm hoping for more awareness of those values and a recognition that those values are historical constructions as opposed to universal measurements of excellence. As John Keene remarks in an essay, "Elements of Literary Style": "No style stands outside the history in which it emerges, or outside the political, social and cultural context in which the author deploys it." He writes that

> a sociocultural asynchrony with the dominant styles in the Anglophone world can present challenges, making the work sound stilted and out of fashion, even though it was written just yesterday and rings with a freshness in its own local context. The easier any literary style is to carry over into English, the more likely it is to be read globally, and perhaps translated into other languages from English.... Yet what about English-language writers themselves, or those writers in other languages who see the unique resources of their native tongues and their national and cultural literary and oral traditions as

a source of strength, artistry, and innovation, as well as
the fount of their distinctive styles?

Among the latter, those writing out of the resources of their own local traditions rather than in a dominant Anglophone style, are Telugu writers. Because their work is not consistent with Anglophone literary values it will be less widely read and more readily dismissed as unmatched for American standards of excellence and American literary taste. It will not be a good fit.

But it is precisely in this moment of democratic crisis in the U.S. that other literatures with their ill-fitting aesthetics and divergent styles might be most necessary for us to encounter. It's a moment when we need to ask ourselves what purpose our literary forms serve in our culture and what else they might serve. If I found myself uncomfortable with the committed writing that I first stumbled upon in Telugu, I was equally discouraged when I was in India in 2014 and I was asked, why after the U.S. had been at war for more than ten years, the war didn't show up in American writing. Why are people still writing about suburban ennui, someone asked me? Why doesn't your literature reflect upon the terrible upheaval your country has created in the world? These were excellent questions, and I had no answer.

These days I ask myself and others, what can writers in the U.S. do with their words to reflect an era in which language is being used as an instrument of unreality? I think one way of seeing what writers might do is to read more works in translation, to read literature that does directly engage social and political issues, and literatures in which writers have a tradition of using irony or contorting language to respond to censorship and authoritarianism. What literature in translation can reveal to us, especially literature that is at odds with our own dominant literary culture, is our blind spots; by engaging radical difference we can find support in the paths—not one but many—writers have blazed through difficult times.

In the end I believe that a tolerance for incongruence can itself be a value both in life and in art. As an immigrant I know that the different languages, ideas, and ways of perceiving and being in the world that have informed me don't add up to a harmonious whole. There are strands of my identity that will never fit well together. The ability to hold divergent and even contradictory ways of looking at a word, a concept, or an attitude, though, can give rise, I think, to a useful skepticism of smug cultural certainties. I don't have a comforting resolution for the conflict between literary values in American and Telugu literature, but the conflict allows me to look at both aesthetic pleasure and literary ethics in each culture more clearly.

When we bring together incongruent works or allow ourselves to be receptive to work that doesn't immediately abide with our conventions, some other way of seeing ourselves or a new form of knowledge can come into being. I recently co-translated short fiction by the feminist Telugu writer, Vimala. After working through the short story "The Dark Girl's Laughter," the story became connected in my mind with Marguerite Duras's novella "The Square." I don't make the comparison with marketing slogans in mind. I don't mean to say, "If you like Marguerite Duras, try Vimala" or "Vimala is the Marguerite Duras of India." The mention of the French writer is not meant to add legitimacy to the Telugu writer. Besides, their styles are distinct. It's that one work made me think of the other. Vimala's story is steeped in the specific caste, gender, class, and cultural concerns of South India, and Duras' story has a more intense despair and existential weight. But both "The Dark Girl's Laughter" and "The Square" provide insight into the lives of dispossessed young women who stubbornly cling to hope when they have no good reason to do so. Both stories lack conventional narrative drive and work instead through a circular and repetitive conversation between two strangers. Each in a different manner says something about the lives of marginalized young women. When I look at Vimala's story in this way, further connections—to Clarice Lispector,

Mercè Rodoreda, Nawal El Sadaawi—come to mind. Through all these writers in translation we have the opportunity not only to witness the narratives of others, but also to put those narratives in conversation with our own. In reading others what we gain is not simply more company, but an experience of solidarity.

Silence, Exile,
and Translating

BRADLEY SCHMIDT

*That's everything I wanted to take care of here. When I turn around one last
time in the front doorway, I see Arnim's gun lying on the kitchen table.
It's enough for me. I don't go back into the kitchen, don't cast a final gaze
into the yard. There's nothing left for me here.*
—Philipp Winkler, *Hooligan*, tr. Bradley Schmidt

*And it never did occur to me to leave 'til tonight
And there's no one left to ask if I'm alright
I'll sleep until I'm straight enough to drive, then decide
If there's anything that can't be left behind*
—Jason Isbell, "Speed Trap Town"

When I first read Philipp Winkler's *Hool* in the original German, I
expected a hard-hitting tale of soccer fans and the crimes—large and
small—committed while doing what they do. But I didn't expect to find
myself. While I grew up chanting *Rock Chalk*, suffering disappointments
every March, I never got in a fight over the Jayhawks. I might have, but
getting into brawls just wasn't one of the ways people supported our
team, especially if raised by pacifists with a penchant for turning the other
cheek. Even diving into Winkler's text for the first time, I had my eyes
on whether or not *I* could write his story, the calm seas and the lurking
cultural icebergs. Writing on Barthes, Susan Sontag notes his passion
for typologies and hones in on a second type of reading: "the pleasure
of reading that is already tormented by the desire to do the same." In a

seeming accident, I am among those granted a special dispensation—permission to do both in translation.

Growing up in rural Kansas, translation didn't seem like an everyday occurrence. At least not "Translation" with a capital T. It was something that I could run across if I got bored with the assigned reading, if I took the teacher's snide remark about the paperback copy of *The Brothers Karamazov* collecting dust in the corner as a challenge, stumbling over the patronymics, the odd words like *samovar*. The evidence was undeniable: translation was something that happened, that took place. But who and where and why were all questions beyond my imagination, my horizon.

If I close my eyes and concentrate, I can still taste it, raw and unpasteurized. I would poke my head into the milking barn, half-heeding the admonishment to stay back, get out while they're working, you don't want to get kicked in the head, do ya? These are some of my first memories. The pungent scent of manure, the fecund earth. The exhaustion on their faces as my grandparents kept trying to eke out a living on the farm. The "home place" is what it was called. My parents and the three of us kids didn't live there because there wasn't enough space, no hope, ain't no future farmin'. A short time after my uncle wrapped his car around a telephone pole, heading back to his job at the meat-packing plant in Dodge City, Grandpa stopped taking me along to the auctions. What's the point of buying heifers if you're thinkin' of quittin'? I strained to catch words, decipher meaning in the auctioneer's chant, two hundred two and a half, two-fifty, how about two-fifty? fifty? fifty? fifty? I got it! How 'bout two-sixty? He taught me to accent the sweetness with something salty. Eatin' watermelon with Saltine crackers, puttin' peanuts in my bottle of Dr. Pepper. We always listened to Paul Harvey's *The Rest of the Story* before the grain prices were read out on the commodities reports.

Because I wanted to find out what the fuss was all about, I broke down and bought a copy of Sebald's *Vertigo*. Went all the way to Barnes and Noble in Wichita. I knew my German wasn't nearly good enough to make heads or tails of the original. The only other association, a vague third-hand recollection, was the title of the old Hitchcock flick. But I'd never seen any of those classics because I didn't grow up with a TV, which would have been "worldly." After all, children needed to be protected from pernicious influences. In a small concession to the outer world, my generation was the first in my Mennonite community that'd been allowed to dance. But visiting the library was encouraged and no one dictated what I could check out. I'd read some Kafka before (in translation, of course) and picked up on the references to "Dr. K" in the Sebald. I asked myself if, in some other world, the pilgrimage to W. could be to my hometown, my W. But of course the mountains I knew were some ten hours due west, sans *Schloss*. And I'd never really felt the dizziness of vertigo, to be honest. Just the woozy feeling after taking too many hits during practice, having been talked into playing eight-man football.

Grandpa managed to keep the farm, but he sold off all the cattle, almost all of the equipment. I remember we still went there on the weekends, got to run around, exploring the overgrown shelterbelt when there weren't any green beans to pick, any weeding to be done. I listened to the stories of the dust bowl, the swarms of locusts. And holding the hoe at precisely the right angle was of utmost importance, shaving the surface of the soil. And then I'd hear the conversations, grandpa chattering away in *Plautdietsch* with some other old farmer. Grandma and me sitting a couple feet away, snapping beans. Once in a while she'd let out a squawk, amused by something she'd overheard. I remember the time Dad helped to load a pig. How they kept slipping in the mud, how for a while, everyone had a grin smeared 'cross their faces. Not becoming what they were, not being tethered to the land was the first failure, the first thing I left behind.

It was obvious from the beginning that manual labor wasn't the answer, wasn't sustainable. After all, my dad had been persuaded to quit welding balers and did enough training to start working at the hospital. After more than five years of managing to not get fired, the logical conclusion was to keep at it, and later have his son become a doctor. If the

Lord was good enough to put a smart head on your shoulders, you were supposed to do something sensible with it. Time, treasures, and talents. So I got to sit in on some surgeries. Managed not to vomit. I needed the cash so I was talked into supplementing my pre-med studies by working as a nurse aide at the old folk's home. Because I needed the cash. Our kind don't go into debt, especially not to the government.

When I did finally make it across the pond, there was a heady mixture of idealism and naïveté. Actually being where Hannah Arendt studied under Heidegger, where Bultmann lectured, where the brothers Grimm, Gadamer, and Bettina von Arnim all spent time. Sure, there was the patina, the cobblestone streets, a palpable sense of history in the air, but more than that, there was the feeling of freedom, trying out ideas, outfits, ideologies without fear of repercussions, escaping the community where everyone knew everyone and nothing went undiscovered. Here I was still crossing lines, even if there were no rules. Not against alcohol, nor for chapel attendance. So I demonstrated against the neo-Nazis, sang the *Internationale*, stayed up late, and let my hair grow out. What would happen if I just stayed? Some of my fellow students had told me about the lack of tuition fees, and I had frugality in my genes, already had some experience subsisting on Ramen instant noodles. And almost by accident, I'd opted out of the best-laid plans; I was never stepping foot in medical school. I simply dropped the pre-med major and never went back—had my German Studies diploma sent to me in the mail.

I'm fond of saying I wear many hats. Which is another way of saying I do more than one thing. Which is another way of saying I can't do just one thing. There's no one thing. Can't fence me in. It does come in handy. Depending on the situation, being able to claim expertise in areas such as translation, German lit, Protestant theology, *drosophila melanogaster*, and yes, I do know how to operate a chainsaw and can make a decent bead with an old stick welder. Usually I just play the role of sincere, overeducated, well-meaning American. But usually that's not even necessary since, including the various alternative spellings, there are nearly half a million people named Schmidt in Germany. Which makes it easy to blend in. After abandoning the white tennis socks and sneakers, and loose-fit jeans, I started to notice how I no longer caught anyone's eye. Pleased to meet you, hope you guess my name. Before I realized it, I was already passing as German.

It's a truism that translations are doomed to failure, are derivative, parasitic. As in: Lost in. Even before Bill Murray and Scarlett Johansson put the phrase back on the pop-cultural map, anyone with any ambition knew it shouldn't be more than a side gig. In *This Little Art*, the revelatory meditation on translation, Kate Briggs recalls a professor's advice: don't do translations; at least not if you're planning to make a living. In fact, literary translation has always been a hobby. Helen Lowe-Porter, whose words are now synonymous with Thomas Mann in the English-speaking word, first took up translation because she "did not want to vegetate intellectually." Equipped with a masters in applied translation, I had acquired a tool kit. I could transform birth certificates, sets of terms and conditions, users manuals for devices manufactured to detect the presence of chemical or nuclear contamination. I was able to pay the bills.

I quickly realized, however, that being a doctoral student in systematic *Theologie* was a whole different ball game. The colloquia, the serious young men (though I was not quite so young anymore, was I?), and the sinking feeling that I was most definitely in over my head. Taking on a topic, in Schleiermacher, that was simultaneously safe and full of landmines. So I set out into the deep, dark woods of the German Enlightenment, searching for philosophical predecessors, lost relatives. Until I noticed my stash of pebbles had long run out and there weren't any crumbs left, either. Sometimes I imagined I'd found a community, a circle of fellow sufferers who knew what it was like. Years later, I would learn to recognize the blessing of receiving a text to form, translate. That the words were already all there and all I had to do was find a way to write it— just in English. But struggling to make progress with the dissertation, I felt smothered by the blank pages, the empty screen. The cursor blinking incessantly like a drip-drip-drip of water on my forehead. The looming prospect of being exposed as an impostor, yet another failure, was hard to shake. And the claustrophobia was real, as were the panic attacks, the sleepless nights. How I dreaded the weekly meetings, the sessions that inevitably culminated in an awkward embrace, my doctoral advisor's paw weirdly lingering on my backside, the walrus whiskers tickling my neck. Long before there was a catchy hashtag to describe it, all semblance of professional distance had been violated. So I managed to find the escape hatch, jump, bid farewell to academic dreams.

The question wasn't so much of how to start, or even of starting at all. Rather, it was more of an issue of working up the courage to show other people what I'd been doing. And I'd been "doing" translations for well over a decade. There is an embarrassing, half-repressed memory of having cribbed the bilingual edition of Rilke in a misguided attempt to impress a girl back home. I had already learned how to find the hardest words, turning them over and over in my mind until they haunted my dreams. But if it wasn't just going to remain a collection of personal scribbles, I was going to have to leave the house. After having chosen the pragmatic, "safe" degree in applied translation, there was no time or money to do a pricy MFA somewhere else. So I hitched rides to Berlin, found a place at the table with people who actually translated books. Mostly women, perhaps ten years older than myself, and with infinitely more experience, wiser by leaps and bounds. I started doing samples, workshopping them with my de facto mentors, and submitting some of the meager results to online journals. After a couple years came the weeklong summer school in England, where I felt surprisingly well-informed among the other students from fancy-pants schools. I returned home and kept on casting out into that small pond, pausing only to put fresh bait on the hook. All told, it took less than five years of nibbles and bites before I reeled in my first contract for a book-length project.

I was fortunate to have several books under my belt by the time *Hooligan* landed in my lap. After processing all the action, the brawls, the drugs, the suicides, and broken dreams, what I noticed first was the lack of. Brand names, fancy cars, cash, hope. I'd worked with the German publisher before and they sent me the galleys long before the book was on anyone's radar. And at first it was just the typical request for ten pages. I didn't get my hopes up too much. Philipp Winkler's novel would go on to win prizes, temporarily shaking up the aesthetic of German prose stylings. And the whole time, it reminded me of always going along thrift-store shopping with my mom. I think maybe that's why I have such a clear memory of my first non-thrift-store purchases, clothes not on sale, bought with my own, hard-earned dollars. Winkler doesn't come right out and say his protagonist is poor. Rather, there are a myriad of small clues, indicators that his characters are lower-middle class at best, struggling to get by. And even before I embraced the labor of making words, of changing words, changing the order of words, shifting cultural references, foreignizing and domesticizing, I was overcome by an intense sense of identification. To be clear, I'd never gotten into an accidental brawl, much less something more organized, but I was reminded of the draining task of eking out a living, just barely scraping by, a state of mind I'd like to believe I'd left behind. That gut feeling that there's nowhere to go and no way out.

For a while, I had been audacious enough to see a role model in James Baldwin. Who knows how I got my hands on a copy of *Go Tell It on the Mountain*, back in Kansas, but it certainly made an impression on me. Identifying the hypocrisy, the self-satisfied religious community. And drawing connections to my parents' dabbling with evangelical congregations, even those featuring Pentecostal fervor. But more importantly, I found out where Baldwin was when he wrote it. In Paris, far away from home. And there was that battered copy of *Portrait of the Artist*. The passage toward the end, where Stephen Daedalus declares "I will try to express myself in some mode of life or art as freely as I can and as wholly as I can, using for my defense the only arms I allow myself to use—silence, exile, and cunning," heavily underlined, and later repeatedly scrawled out on note cards. In light of this, it's far from surprising that I left, stayed away, and didn't go back.

But how to define cunning? And what is silence, anyway? And what is actually gained by exile? What is lost?

And when I think about where I'm from, I catch myself vacillating between the urge to distance myself—not just geographically—from the backwater, podunk place hidden behind the wheat fields, and a kind of survivor's guilt. To be perfectly clear: I am not equivocating growing up poor and later becoming a part of a different and socioeconomic class with having survived a natural disaster, genocide, or war. I frequently feel highly ambiguous about my identity, feel torn by conflicting loyalties. Whose story am I telling and for whom am I telling it? Although I feel a strong affinity for Grace Paley, I have felt inhibited, even unable to evoke my ancestors as she does, my rural past cast with a different sheen than stories from the Old Country. And I no longer inhabit the world I grew up in. In *Reading Classes*, the psychologist Barbara Jensen notes many class crossovers or class migrants sense that upward mobility of transitioning into the upper-middle class, hyper-educated milieus often leads to a devaluing of the people and the perspectives left behind. When individuals from my current cohort rant and rave about the ignorant people in the flyover states who vote against their own interests, they don't know it, but they're also railing against me. And I usually fall silent, say nothing. After all, who wants to be associated with those people? How could I own up to feeling a sense of loss for something I gladly cast off?

If I learned anything in my three years toiling away on the never-completed dissertation, it was how to wear a suit coat, take on another skin, how to blend in. Not just be overly educated, but to play the part. Dropping the strong r's of the rural Midwest, I attempted to de-hickify myself. I went from a family of teetotalers to being able to hold my liquor, distinguishing between levels of tannins and minerality. I learned when to laugh and how to make clever references in two language without breaking a sweat. It was a boys club and I knowingly accepted the advantages afforded by my new role. If asked about my past, I dropped names from Marburg, or obfuscated by offering generalities about a private liberal arts college. The German heritage in America was broad enough to not give away my rural roots. In short, I learned to pass as educated, upper-middle class.

To the extent that it is a subject of interest, the role of translation is often projected onto an abstract plane. Frequently invisible, translators can be considered neutral, objective servants performing a small, but necessary role to make literature accessible in another language. But literary translations aren't churned out by machines (yet). As Kate Briggs aptly notes, the translator is a maker of wholes, but knows that the work she is translating is not hers: she knows that it didn't originate with her. On some level, it is irrelevant whether the translator chooses to identify with the author or with the text. Even the presumptive identification does not guarantee that true closeness will arise. But sometimes a text challenges that special reader—who is the translator—and changes something, shifts the emotional architecture. We are by no means empty vessels, and the acts of reading and then having the gall to write it all again using words that are our own—but ultimately remain the author's—is not always uplifting. This shapeshifting often means that, only after having words do something to us as readers, we are able to do something with words. To rend the fabric of the text, then to render, to make something anew, whole.

Literature is capable of many things, but its loftiest effects are tied to its ability to do things to readers, despite writers' claims that they are merely playing with words. When a well-written text falls on fertile soil, it can not only build worlds, working with associations and inspiration, it can also trigger emotions, responses that move beyond the typical pleasure of reading. This is one reason why readers, immersed in books, are able to not only feel so strongly about what they're reading, but also have such strong emotions while talking to others about the books. Typing these lines in fits and starts, stumbling, stuttering, then giving in and sobbing until the screen goes blurry, I remember how I, too, had traveled far. To be sure, Walton, Kansas, is no W., is no Wunsdorf—I can and do go back. And I've never been in a literal fight worth mentioning. There are so many ways that the worlds I have experienced are different than the one in *Hooligan*. But reading and writing a story about a working class hero, I was forced to remember. To feel things I'd long forgotten, repressed, ignored. By then, I was quite accustomed to slipping into new roles, aping different authorial voices, and drawing out narrative threads foreign to myself. But once in this role, I was thrust into a world with such harsh emotional familiarity that I couldn't avoid looking back. I had long sensed there was nothing there I couldn't leave behind, but only while translating a brutal novel about German hooligans did it occur to me that none of it had truly left me.

Collaboration

HEATHER CLEARY

It might seem counterintuitive to talk about collaboration as the future of translation. Translation is, and always has been, an art of making connections: it is a prismatic form of writing grounded in the intersection of languages and cultures (and with them, different subjectivities, worldviews, uses of form, and so on), made possible by a literal or metaphorical dialogue between an author and a translator— the co-elaboration of a text. But there are other ways to think about collaboration in the context of translation, ways that focus less on the cultural and aesthetic dimensions of the practice and more on the ways translation exists within an interconnected system of institutions. As translation scholar Michael Cronin suggests in "A New Ecology for Translation? Collaboration and Resilience," the "local and global dimensions to struggles for language and translation rights are reinforcing one another in the context of a political ecology of translation, adding a further meaning to the notion of 'collaborative' translation." But what is at stake in these language and translation rights if we take the latter term to encapsulate, among other things, both the right of translators to adequate compensation for their labor, and the right of translation to its due recognition in the pantheon of literary arts? How might these rights best be attained, and what do we stand to gain by incorporating various forms of collaboration into our thinking about translation and our communities?

As most translators who have collaborated on an entire book or in workshops and informal exchanges will attest, there is much to recommend working together this way. First and foremost, translation consolidates the original text according to a specific interpretation at a specific moment in time, so it follows that much could be gained from forming that interpretation in dialogue with another close reader of the work (and no reader gets closer than a translator). Though this distinction sometimes blurs upon close inspection, I'm not talking about models of "collaboration" that involve a speaker of the source language producing a trot, or literal translation, that is later "turned into art" by the credited translator of the work—a dynamic reminiscent of the colonialist logic of the native informant, and not part of any future I would advocate. I am thinking, instead, of four-handed translations, projects undertaken by two translators who approach the undertaking as equals, and which are refined by an ongoing exchange that brings multiple interpretations and translational toolkits to bear in rendering the work. As Emma Ramadan wrote in the *Quarterly Conversation* on her experience collaborating on various translations, there is "something incredibly comforting about a co-translation. Someone else has validated your choices, someone else has said 'this is a good idea,' the potential of being scoffed at has been reduced." Ultimately, "half the fun of co-translating is being able to witness the other person's process, hear their thoughts, watch as they replace words with others that feel more right—or at least less wrong— struggling and breaking through together." In her candid assessment of the doubts and delights that translation inspires, Ramadan points to an important truth of collaboration: there are many different kinds of strength in numbers—including, but not limited to, guarding against the interpretive blind spots and linguistic tics to which we are all individually subject.

Of course, conditions are not always favorable for formal co-translations: though there have been many notable exceptions— including but not limited to Ramadan's recent experiences, Lisa Dillman and Daniel Hahn's work with Eduardo Halfon (the team for *The Polish*

Boxer included Anne McLean, Ollie Brock, and Thomas Bunstead, as well), and the dynamic duo of Russian retranslation, Larissa Volokhonsky and Richard Pevear—this kind of collaboration tends to meet resistance from publishers. The easiest explanation for this is that it is simply not financially expedient to hire two people for a job that, presumably, one could do alone. Fair enough: in many cases, a formal co-translation would probably be overkill on several levels. Nonetheless, a reason often given (based on personal experience and anecdotal evidence) for not wanting to publish co-translations is the fear of "a lack of cohesion," or concern that the final product will end up like Frankenstein's monster: stitched together from mismatched parts, intelligible to no one.

I find this argument particularly interesting because it seems to be grounded in the effacement of several ways in which the translator's voice is already polyphonous: as I mentioned above, it will always at the very least be in conversation with that of the author (even, I would argue, in the case of self-translation). The most likely scenario, however, is that there will be other people involved in the exchange, including an editor who might bring an entirely different set of criteria to the table. The notion of the translator as the privileged diviner of a stable and cohesive original text seems linked, moreover, to the individualistic cult of ingenuity so deeply entrenched in our cultural, political, and economic institutions—a fetish that tends to efface the networks of support that create the conditions of possibility for any significant achievement. For all these reasons, I would underscore the value of collaboration in translation as we move forward, whether formally (a pair or team of translators working together on an entire book) or informally (translators trading insights and helping to refine one another's projects). Personally, I've found these informal exchanges to be invaluable; for the past year or so I've been participating in small workshops with friends who also translate from Spanish into English. Our shared knowledge of the literary context our projects come from, not to mention some of the typical linguistic snares (and solutions) specific to our language pair, has benefitted the projects enormously, and also given each of us a range of new tools with which to approach future translations. Ultimately, not only are these forms of collaboration likely to offer a richer vision of the text than might have been possible otherwise, they also draw our attention away from the myth of the lone genius and toward the material reality of bringing out a book, which almost always involves discussion, debate, and compromise within an institutional framework.

Branching out from the textual models of collaboration outlined above, there is a growing number of professional or semi-professional organizations—like ALTA, the PEN Translation Committee, and ELTNA, a network for emerging literary translators in the United States, among others—that foster collaboration and in many cases aim to mitigate the isolation and precarity that freelancers (like translators) can often experience. These advocacy groups not only offer vital resources like an annual conference where translators can gather to share stories, new projects, and advice, but also robust lists of funding opportunities and residencies, and a meticulously prepared model contract. ELTNA (inspired by the Emerging Translator's Network, or ETN, in the U.K.) offers an online forum for those new to the field, as well as mentorship from those more established in the field. ALTA has also developed an extensive mentorship program with a special focus on underrepresented languages. Though both formal and informal mentorship have long played an important role in the field of translation, an essential part of the future lies here: in actively fostering translations from languages and perspectives that have not historically had the same degree of visibility in English, produced by increasingly diverse generations of translators.

Another promising mode of collaboration in translation is that of the collective. Several of these groups have formed over the past year, including Third Coast Translator Collective, Emerging Translators Collective, and others here in the States, as well as The Starling Bureau in the U.K. Each of these organizations has its own focus and its own mission, but all emphasize resource sharing among their members and outreach that involves public readings, consulting services for the publishing industry, and more. The Emerging Translators Collective produces broadsides and chapbooks as a way of subverting not only the restrictive nature of the publishing industry, but also the economic model on which it is based. Their mission statement reads:

> If we are to take translation, as praxis, seriously, then we need to understand that the current market doesn't necessarily reflect the interests of translators, despite the fact that lofty ideas of world literature are realized through their bodies. Even those who claim to be indexes of world literature participate in an uneven system of global cultural production and dissemination. In brief, we aim to foster a sharing of knowledge without claims to possession.

Like many of its sister organizations, the Emerging Translators Collective is both inward- and outward-facing, both seeking to improve the conditions under which its members practice translation, and also thinking about the place translation and its practitioners hold in the cultural system of which they form part.

Cedilla & Co., of which I am a member, came into being in 2016, when Julia Sanches and Sean Gasper Bye started thinking about why representation from an agent is not an available or desirable option for most translators, and what could be done within the community to provide some of the support an agent would provide—not for a percentage taken against an advance, but rather on the basis of a barter economy. Before long, we'd become a group of nine translators working from ten different languages. We meet regularly to discuss individual projects and industry news: one of the key functions of the collective is to offer support with refining pitch materials, collectively brainstorming submission lists, and providing introductions with editors as appropriate. Once a project is picked up, we also provide a sounding board for contract negotiations, basing our feedback on both the excellent PEN model contract and our own experience. In this way, we not only help one another advocate for ourselves in these discussions, but also collectively develop ways to effectively communicate what the art-and-labor of translation entails during the contract negotiation process. Within the broader literary community, Cedilla provides reader reports to editors and helps them contextualize projects of interest from areas where we have expertise. In this way, the collective hopes to make the acquisition of works in translation less daunting and grounded more solidly in the specificity of the literary traditions involved. Cedilla also holds readings on a regular basis to showcase projects for the publishing industry and to present work in translation in an accessible format to the public at large.

Finally, underscoring the political dimensions of translation in all its diverse forms and related practices, Antena is a community-centered collective dedicated to language justice and experimentation. Founded in 2010 by writer-translator-interpreters Jen Hofer and John Pluecker (in 2014 a locally focused collective took shape in Los Angeles, and in 2015 another was formed in Houston), and guided by the principle that "language is a tool for empowering thinking and transforming action," Antena combines translation projects with site-specific multilingual interventions and social justice interpreting work. On the literary end of the spectrum, Antena's members engage in the kind of collaborative translation outlined above—while finding ways to put their own spin on the process and final product. Most recently, in 2017 Les Figues Press published Myriam Moscona's *Tela de sevoya / Onioncloth*, a collaborative translation credited first and foremost to Antena with Hofer and Pluecker's names listed in parenthesis after that of the organization.

Antena also has its own publishing operation: under the imprint Libros Antena Books, the collective produces a series of pamphlets and chapbooks that includes *A Manifesto for Ultratranslation* (available as a free PDF on their website). The manifesto is essential reading for thinking through and beyond visibility to the ethical future of translation, where this future interacts with social and cultural practice, and how we might get there. "Ultratranslation," begins one entry,

> labors to translate the untranslatable, and also to preserve it: not to reduce the irreducible. Not to know but to acknowledge. Ultratranslation does not replace translation, nor does it seek to depose. They exist beside one another and concurrently, one feeding the other. Two bodies with the negative space of relation between them. Only in the geography of the margins, in the space between, only there. Ultratranslation is not translation unmoored from meaning, but translation that questions what and how meaning itself means.

From the simultaneous presence of multiple languages in a physical space of encounter, to the simultaneous presence of the translated text and the trace of its original—of rendering and the rejection of appropriation—Antena's practice and manifesto present a continuum of coexistence and collaboration that might serve as a guide as we think about, and move into, the future of translation.

I hope this incomplete list provides a sense of some of the vital collaborations already working to strengthen the translator's position within the publishing industry, and that it might help us develop new ways to think and talk about both our art and our labor. I also hope it inspires more projects in a similar vein. Because by forming a collective body, we make ourselves easier to see, and by finding practical, ethically sound ways to push back against the "liberal, utilitarian paradigm" that, as Cronin writes, privileges individualism over "the collective embrace of the relational that is seen as part of the utopian project of translation," we not only improve our working conditions, we also guide translation toward its best future. Books are a business, of course, and of course the publishers of books in translation, who are our allies in this, are restricted by financial considerations and often have to make choices they might rather not. But the more we translators are able to develop strategies to work both within and around the established structures of the industry, the more we are able to pool our intellectual and experiential resources, and the more we actively seek to expand the translation community by opening it to a broader range of perspectives, languages, and practitioners, the stronger both we and our work will be.

O
F

T
R
A
N
S
L
A
T
I
O
N

Writing the Reality We Want
A Conversation on Some Potentials of Translation

LUCAS KLEIN AND ELEANOR GOODMAN

LUCAS KLEIN: What will the future bring when it comes to translation? I think of what critic and translator Eliot Weinberger wrote thirty years ago: "The two golden ages of English-language poetry (roughly 1550 to 1650 and 1910 to when? 1970?) were not coincidentally eras of intense translating." Listing, with ease, all the poets and novelists from that second golden age who published significant works of translation, he added that "the difficult list to make is those who never translated poetry." In contrast, he said, since the seventies there were "only two 'avant-garde' poets who continue to translate regularly"—Rosmarie Waldrop and Clayton Eshleman. "Only a few others have done occasional translations. What has happened?"

"In an era of rampant nationalism and xenophobia," Weinberger answered, even the ostensibly left-wing poets stopped translating: "Reaganism has infected every particle of life in this country, not excluding the life and work of poets, no matter how much they may hold in him contempt." More recently, though, in a piece called "Anonymous Sources," he's taken up another point: "Translation liberates the translation-language, and it is often the case that translation flourishes when the writers feel that their language or society needs liberating." So if in the sixties translation was "an act of defiance against the government," the "first years of the twenty-first century have seen a boom in new presses that publish translation, grants and prizes, courses in translation, international festivals, websites," he writes. "Once again, Americans were ashamed to be American, were fed up with America, and began looking abroad just to hear the sound of someone else's voice."

We can now indeed think of more than just Eshleman and Waldrop among North American poets who translate—Anne Carson, Peter Cole, Forrest Gander, Erín Moure, Cole Swensen, and Jeffrey Yang come to mind, without putting much thought into it, as do Jen Hofer and Johannes Göransson—and you, of course, Eleanor. But now that we are in an era of even more nationalism and xenophobia than Reagan's, what can we expect to happen to the relationship between poetry and translation? Will there be more poets translating, or are we building a wall between native and foreign while trying to make American poetry great again?

ELEANOR GOODMAN: We very clearly are "in an era of rampant nationalism and xenophobia," and not just here in the U.S. or in the English-speaking world. It seems natural that translation would then become more undervalued than it has been, even as it underpins everything from our basic education (who doesn't read something in translation in school, often without being told that it was written first in another language?) to our business dealings to global politics. Still, I see another interesting phenomenon going on, which has been commented on in other contexts, namely multilingual books. The case I'm thinking of specifically is a book by Juan Felipe Herrera, *Notes on the Assemblage*, in which several poems appear in both English and Spanish. I initially assumed that the poems were translated by the author himself, but in the acknowledgements at the very end of the book, Herrera thanks Lauro Flores "for translating a number of these poems into Spanish." I take that to mean that the poems in Spanish in the volume are by Flores? And it makes me wonder about a poem like "Borderbus," which involves a lot of Spanish mixed in with the English—who wrote the Spanish, and is it a translation of an original English text? Do these questions even matter?

On the opposite side of that particular spectrum is the brilliant book *Alice Iris Red Horse* by Yoshimasu Gōzō, edited by Forrest Gander, in which translators and the act of translation are made as transparent as possible: each translation is prefaced by "translator's notes" that bring us into the translator's creative process and foreground all of the minute and continuous decisions that are being made throughout the reading, interpreting, writing, and revising involved in translation. Everything is explicitly laid out on the page, there for the reader to explore. As Gander puts it in his introduction: "Some readers may question whether these innovative translations represent the original. But I wonder if the goal of 'representing' the original is the goal of translation at all, given that the work is necessarily subjected to alteration, transformation, dislocation, and displacement."

While these two examples strike me as coming at the issue from very different angles, the point is that neither of these texts are purely English texts, and neither are purely translations. After postmodernism, when the authority of the writer has been undermined completely, maybe we're moving into a stage in which the distinctions between translator and writer, or original and translation, are being blurred to the point of disappearing.

LK: Maybe we're moving into a stage in which the distinctions between original and translation are being blurred to the point of disappearing. Is that a direction we want to move in?

Rigid distinctions and sharp borders can do a lot of damage, and challenging them even at the level of literature and translation may help us reach an understanding of interconnectedness. If we stop looking for definitive versions, right answers at the exclusion of other valid interpretations, and dogmatism, we might be able to build on such attitudes of accommodation as foundations for peace. We can appreciate that translation requires creativity, as does poetry, so what's the difference? On the other hand, there's a lot of anxiety about "fake news" and whether we're "post-truth" right now, and if we overwrite all translations as simply "renditions" or "versions" of a source text that doesn't really exist, then we may not be modeling good behavior for other areas of our life. If part of the goal of translation is to write against xenophobia by bringing the foreign into our poetry, will multilingual poetry that works via code-switching, say, get us to the same place as the painstaking process of giving writers from other places and times a voice in a language we can understand? A poem with lines in both English and Spanish can't but occur differently to me, because I don't know Spanish, than a poem that recreates in English what another poem in Spanish says and does. If the distinction between original and translation is blurred to the point of disappearing, then at one level what's "lost in translation" is *translation.*

One way to answer that is to realize that while you say this occurs "after postmodernism," it isn't that new of a phenomenon. Weinberger's lists, alluded to above, include Ezra Pound, of course, whose poems are famously (or infamously) polylingual, and Louis Zukofsky, whose homophonic *Catullus* cannot be appreciated without at least sounding out the Latin on which it's based. And prior to that, when the classes who might be expected to care about philological accuracy in translation could instead be expected to know the languages being translated—Greek, Latin, and French, at least—there would have been much blurring of distinctions between translator and writer. For instance, I learned recently that *Romeo and Juliet* is a theatrical adaptation of a 1562 poem by Arthur Brooke based on Pierre Boaistuau's French rendering of a novella by Italian Matteo Bandello. I think it would be great if we started bringing our blurring of distinctions between translator and writer, or original and translation, to bear on Shakespeare. We don't do that, I think, because we are still in the thrall of Shakespeare as "genius" *par excellence.* But also, we'd be missing something if we rubbed out all the distinctions of the translational process that gets us from Bandello to *Romeo and Juliet* and what we now think of as translation proper.

To put it concretely, if you were going to teach a class on Dante, would you assign your students Mary Jo Bang's *Inferno?* It begins:

Stopped mid-motion in the middle
Of what we call our life, I looked up and saw no sky—
Only a dense cage of leaf, tree, and twig. I was lost.

It's difficult to describe a forest:
Savage, arduous, extreme in its extremity. I think
And the facts come back, then the fear comes back.

Death, I believe, can only be slightly more bitter.
I can't address the good I found there
Until I describe in detail what else I saw.

Contrast this with what Burton Raffel gives:

Halfway along the road of this our life
    I woke to find myself in a wood so dark
        That straight and honest ways were gone, and light
Was lost. O, how hard to tell the harsh
    Horror of that wild and brutal forest!
        The very thought brings back a fear so stark
That bitter death itself seems not much worse.
    But let me tell the rest of what I met with,
        So the good I found is well and truly rehearsed.

There are as many similarities as differences between their renditions. Both are interpretations of Dante's Italian, after all. But which sounds more like what we can appreciate as the voice of a medieval Florentine, writing in *terza rima*? Most of us would be happy calling them both "versions," even "adaptations," but some would bristle at the idea that Bang's is a *translation*.

Then again, maybe the mind-set of a teacher is not the best (or only) mind-set we should adopt here. I don't have a problem with Bang's version. I used to edit a literary journal devoted to translations and versions that played with our understanding of translation in just such ways. And think about what Caroline Bergvall does in *Via: 48 Dante Variations*, quoting so many translations of the first stanza of the *Inferno*. But I also think that we can appreciate Bang's version more if we have less on-the-surface "free" translations to balance it against. The way that we can appreciate Baz Luhrmann's 1996 *Romeo + Juliet* more—or can appreciate *West Side Story* more—if we've seen other versions of the play with different dramaturgy. So while there's something exciting about blurring the line between "original" and "translation" sometimes, there's a real value in maintaining that line, too.

EG: I think one of the main points you've made beautifully here is that the author of a text should be very clear as to what that text is, what it is intended to do, and how she is going to do it. Then we as readers can decide whether we want to read it, whether we're enjoying reading it for what it is, and whether in the end the author has succeeded in producing a text that does what it advertises. The problem with blurring the lines between translation and recreation and free imitation is that the reader can end up feeling cheated. At least I as a reader certainly can, and do. I want to know if what I'm reading has come from a foreign language and culture and hews closely to it, or if has been heavily filtered the lens of the target language and culture. I think work that doesn't make the distinction clear is on some level disingenuous. It's a case of false advertising. Having said that, I don't know exactly where these lines should be drawn, and I very much hesitate to draw any definitive lines at all. Every text is different, every translator is different, and as translation theory shows us, there are nearly as many translation techniques as there are texts to translate. But as a working translator, I feel pretty clear about when I'm deviating from a text (plain old errors aside), and when I'm sticking very close to the original intent as I perceive it. For example, I sometimes add a little bit of information into a text if there's a reference I think Western readers are unlikely to get just as is—like adding the word "emperor" onto a name. It can be dangerous to do that, but I often don't want to create a mystery where there isn't one in the original. I wonder if you feel that way too.

I also think that this is all connected to the fact that translators tend to get hidden by original authors, so that maybe in the general reading population, there isn't a lot of clarity about who has done what. If we can still be publishing books without the translator's name on the cover, that to me is an indication that our literary culture is lamentably behind the times in this respect—and that's all without bringing up the 3 percent bugbear. I hope that going forward, we can think of a translator's oeuvre, and place books within that rubric, rather than thinking about translated works as essentially belonging to the original author at the expense of the translator. Someone like, say, Andrea Lingenfelter or Nicky Harman deserves to have her books thought of as forming a collective whole, and each new translation viewed and reviewed partly from that perspective. I wonder if this seems to contradict what I was saying before—I do indeed think of translation as an act of creation and the work of the translator above all. I don't want to dictate the choices that are on the table for translators, and those that are not. I simply want to know what I'm getting when I pick up a book.

LK: Yes, translators like Lingenfelter and Harman deserve their translations collected under their names. And it's not unheard of: Peter Cole, mentioned above, has published a recent book with the subtitle *New and Selected Poems and Translations*, potentially putting his own poems and his translations of others' poems on equal footing. And as a book buyer I've done similar things: I'd never heard of Julio Cortázar before coming across *Hopscotch* in a bookstore one time, but I bought the book because I saw that it was translated by Gregory Rabassa, and I trusted the taste and skill of the translator who had also given us Gabriel García Márquez's *One Hundred Years of Solitude*. In fact, this is my argument about why translators should have our names on book covers: if actors can have their names on movie posters, can't we also brand our names to promote our work? It's another way to market the literature in question.

But again, there's another side to that—which does not necessarily involve queasiness about capitalism (though there's room for that, too!). One of the reasons I translate is to step out of myself, to turn the selflessness of giving into something like egolessness. If Lingenfelter or Harman have similar attitudes toward the implicit spirituality of translation, collecting all their translations under their names might create for us a context that prompts us to see their artistry at the expense of the artistry of the work being translated (rather than the two united as one). And whatever else that does, it might also muddy the transparency you want about what a text is, what it's intended to do, and how it's going to be done.

EG: There is definitely something to the idea of a selfless translation/translator. But I think it's potentially a dangerous idea as well. I think Emily Wilson—whom I admire tremendously—articulates it perfectly when she says in an interview with Channel 4 news, apropos her new translation of the *Odyssey*:

> I've certainly been shocked to realize how much there are visible misogynies that are not just from one or another translator but multiple translators... There's never a definitive translation and a translator always makes choices. What I am objecting to is that people tend to think of other translations as: "They didn't make choices, they just wrote what was in the Greek." Everybody makes choices.

Certainly in this context, where we're looking at inherited prejudices, it's important to realize that every translator comes at a text from his or her own era, as well as from his or her own particular angle, including biases and other nasty influences that enter the text. If we think of the translator as "egoless," and in that sense pure or some kind of uncomplicated vehicle, then I think we risk overlooking these very important elements (or "deforming tendencies" as Antoine Berman puts it, in Venuti's translation) that inevitably color a translation.

Having said that, I know that we're both very aware of our own influence on the texts we translate, as any good translator is. And the attempt to reach toward a kind of selflessness I think is still an important gesture in many (though clearly not all) cases: it is something to aim for, if not something that can necessarily ever be achieved.

LK: I'm glad you mentioned Wilson. I haven't read her *Odyssey*, but I think the discourse around it is one of the most promising things to have happened in the field of literary translation recently: there seems to be the possibility of an intelligent public discussion about the role of the translator in shaping how we read texts from other places and times—in this case, specifically, how the translator does or does not relay or replay sexism in the representation of that text. Another example I came across recently is Stephanie McCarter's piece in *Electric Literature*, "Rape, Lost in Translation: How Translators of Ovid's *Metamorphoses* Turn an Assault into a Consensual Encounter." In fact, I don't know how receptive anyone would have been to McCarter's points without Wilson first. What Wilson has brought to the fore (again) is that translation is an inherently political act, even or especially when it deals with texts we usually think of as nonpolitical. How do you as translator represent the reality of the source text as you observe it, and use it responsibly to write the reality you want? That isn't an easy question, for political activists or for translators, but it is, I think, the one we have to ask. And Wilson gives me hope that the book-reading public can be brought into that discussion and understand its stakes for literature and for building a future for all of us.

As for what Wilson says about decision-making—with which I agree—and the selflessness of the translator, I'd like to imagine that we can transcend our egos and make decisions at the same time. That's not straightforward to put into practice, but making decisions based not only on our own senses of self, but rather out of responsibility for others, could be an important step in realizing it. Sometimes when people talk about translational selflessness it sounds pathological, or else like some kind of expression of a martyr complex (along the lines of, *The translator is only noticed when something's wrong*). But what I have in mind here is a kind of meeting of Zen and communalism: I make the decisions that constitute this translation, but they are made in what I take to be the interests of the community as a whole, to best represent the work of literature as a piece of public property. So while they are made by me, they are more precisely made by that sense of responsibility.

EG: Yes, I think a sense of responsibility is key—to the text, to our readers, and ultimately to ourselves. In this respect, translators are no different from any other kind of author, and can fall into all of the same kinds of traps: cliché, unintentional lack of clarity, dull language, problematic prejudices, laziness of many different kinds. I hope, contrary to our pessimism at the beginning of this conversation, that as we muddle our way through this particular historical moment we can continue to push our culture forward toward a broadening of awareness instead of a contraction. Translation, and the contact with foreign ideas, habits, roles, worldviews, values, philosophies, daily lives, etc., that translation brings, can be part of the way out of this horrifically myopic and destructive moment that we're in. I certainly think of my translation work as in part a political act. It is bringing "the sound of someone else's voice," as Weinberger puts it, to a literary culture that can be pretty insular and solipsistic. We have a long way to go, but in the end I believe that what translators do really does make a difference.

Impossible Connections

BONNIE CHAU

I have told this story before: *I really kind of believe that translation is going to save the world*, I say. Sometimes this is how I begin the story; sometimes this is how I end the story. If, sometime in the past several years, you and I have just met, and for whatever reason we have found ourselves in informal and spirited conversation about translation, and especially if I sense in you a latent interest or burgeoning curiosity, I most likely have said these words to you, maybe I have even lowered my voice to fervently whisper them to you: *I really kind of believe that translation is going to save the world.*

2014: The beginning: In my second semester of grad school, I decided to take a translation workshop for fun. I'd known when entering into the Columbia MFA program that it had a translation track (LTAC) because I had read through every inch of its website when I was applying to schools, but I was surprised to encounter people who had selected the program precisely because it had such a track. In 2014, I was thirty-two, and somehow it had never occurred to me, even as someone raised in a Chinese-speaking household, even as someone who had attended Chinese-language school for thirteen years, even as someone who had lived and taught English in France for two years, it had never occurred to me to be interested in translation.

I have told this story before. In this story that I tell, in the way that I've told it, it seems startlingly illogical and inexplicable, a total fluke, that despite all of these factors, *it had somehow never occurred to me.* A stroke of unfortunate luck, like not thinking to bring an umbrella. It is occurring to me only now that this was not some inexplicable absentmindedness, some mental blip, this translation-shaped hole, this blind spot in which the wound of translation stood seething but unseen. In Johannes Göransson's "Translation Wounds," (part of his and Joyelle McSweeney's *Deformation Zone* manifesto) translation is a wound, and I am immediately pulled into this figuration as I begin examining why translation for me feels like an insistent widening of a wound in my self. It is the wound itself, and also an active wounding process—that tunnels into and through the body (of text)—producing openings and holes. I force myself inside the wound, continually creating the wound. It occurs to me now, it has been *occurring* to me, that there are reasons, a logical continuity, to my journey toward and through translation, to my tunneling.

Such as: As a Chinese American person growing up in a bilingual Chinese- and English-speaking household in Irvine, California, in the 1980s, attending my 95 percent white elementary school, I spent as many hours Sunday mornings at Chinese school, as I did hours of my own conscious and subconscious time building up an antipathy to the language that set me apart.

Such as: During college in 2003, when friends took Asian American studies courses, or joined Asian student associations or sororities, I remained resolutely skeptical. Why would I want any of those things? Why would I ever choose to take an Asian American studies course? I already had a couple of decades of experience and knowledge of being Asian American under my belt, and let me tell you what I already knew and didn't need to learn in a class: it sucked. I didn't fit in with the fobs, I didn't fit in with the super smart math and science nerds, I didn't fit in with the Asian gangstas, or the Korean kids who all went to church together, or the trio of punk-skater-goth Asian kids. And anyway, why even say Asian American? It seemed desperate and unnecessary to me: when the world saw me it only saw me as an Asian person, and when the world asked me what I was, all I was was Chinese. What the world asked of me essentially was the response that I was something else, something other, and so that was what I would give it, a terse, one-word response. What are you. Chinese. No one really cared for me to say any more than that, to say, oh I'm Chinese *American*.

In fact, even if I was asked to say more, I didn't know how to say it, what to call it. Diaspora, in the sense that I feel inextricably connected to but separate and distant from an ancestral homeland, that has always, even years before I ever visited, shaped my identity and made it impossible to accept that being American is complete enough of an identity for me? Chinese or Asian or second-generation diaspora? Bicultural, transcultural, third-culture kid? It is some sort of shape-shifting space, this very compounding, of Asian, and American. It is a knowing and willful straddling of the space in between, or the space that contains both, that is a manifestation of the movement and migration of people, cultures, languages.

2008: Los Angeles: A lesson in the hierarchy of languages. In many ways I'd already learned this, had been learning it all my life as a native Chinese speaker. What languages and accents are portrayed in media as attractive and sexy? As a high schooler deciding what language to take, obviously I wasn't going to choose Chinese; I was still going to and hating my Sunday mornings at Chinese school. I took Latin for a day, and then switched over to French, where I stayed for the next four years. The more overt lesson, then, in Echo Park, years later, in 2008: I worked at a creative writing/ literary nonprofit whose educational programming predominantly served the neighborhood youth population, most of whom came from Spanish-speaking households. Almost all of the unpaid interns I interviewed and hired, most of them from or attending universities in Southern California, had, like me, chosen either French, Italian, or German as their secondary languages.

Why do we choose the languages we choose? Sometimes on a whim. Sometimes with our eyes closed. Sometimes we have no choice. Sometimes you are born into a language and you spend a long time wishing you had a choice, because if you did, you would not choose it. Think of Deborah

Smith, who in an interview with Allie Park at KTLIT.com talks about her personal chronology of 1) first being interested, generally, in translation work, and then 2) finding Korea to be perfect because it has a flourishing publishing industry but its literature is undertranslated, and then 3) deciding to learn Korean. Smith says, "I had no prior connection with, or investment in, Korea or Korean culture." Think of Benjamin Moser, who writes in the *New York Times*: "My freshman year, I'd abandoned studying Chinese when our professor said it'd be ten years before we'd be able to decipher a newspaper. I switched to Portuguese, despite zero knowledge of the language or culture." And is reported to have said at an event, "Portuguese class was at 11:30 in the morning, making it easier to study." I try to imagine the freedom, the neutrality, of such decision-making when it comes to language, to translation. To simply attach oneself to a language, without the burden of sharing a history with it. I find myself feeling envy, but with a tinge of uneasiness, a feeling that if I keep digging, I would uncover unproductive feelings of anger and contempt, at the systems of power and privilege that have allowed and supported and upheld the projects and publications of generations of white translators over anyone else. Perhaps there is a very specific freedom to being able to choose a language simply because its literature is undertranslated, or because the class time allowed you to sleep in, but could it really be possible to choose a language, whether Korean or Portuguese or Chinese or anything else, completely neutrally?

For many of us in the U.S., we choose a language to study in high school, we choose a language to study in college. Why did I choose French? My sister had taken French in high school and college, my mother had taken French in community college continuing-education classes, we had traveled to France multiple times as a family, we were a family of Francophiles, that's why. But why were we? Oftentimes we choose a language because we admire the literature or culture of that country or region. For many years, I assumed this admiration was neutral enough. But, more recently, in the last ten years or so, I have been learning otherwise. Think of: that lesson I had in the hierarchy of languages back in L.A. Think of: the years I spent teaching in France—many of the other English-language teaching assistants were American and British, many of them had studied or majored in French in college, almost all of them white, upper-middle class, many of the Americans were from the East Coast, New England region. Think of: an admiration built on layers and layers and centuries and centuries of implicit and explicit biases, see: imperialism, neoimperialism, colonialism, neocolonialism.

Back to 2014: In my first translation workshop at Columbia with Susan Bernofsky, I had no idea what to translate. Or what to translate from. We went around the room and introduced ourselves and our language(s). Perhaps motivated by the fact that about half of the people in the room had said they would be translating from French, and that I felt for sure my French skills were subpar anyway, I said French and added on that I might try Chinese. I had no idea how I might try to translate anything from Chinese. Sure I had attended all those years of Chinese school, but I had willfully learned almost nothing, had, especially in the last couple of years, ditched class all the time. I couldn't even read a newspaper, not even close. Supposedly you need to know two to three thousand Chinese characters to read a newspaper; I had no idea how many characters I knew, but it felt more like, I don't know, a couple hundred. But I put it out there, because it was something else at least. French, I said, and maybe I'll try some Chinese. It felt strange, saying that. In the way that these systems of imperialism and neoimperialism have twisted us, it felt like I might be overstepping, the notion that I might be someone who knew anything about Chinese, I, who had skipped out on all those Chinese classes. As if I might dare to put myself into the category of people who translate from Chinese literature that, as far as I knew, consisted solely of old white men in academia. As if I was trespassing on their territory.

In my own writing, as in my own life, my tendencies lean toward the oblique, the elliptical, perhaps a bit of dry humor. What I like to think of as a sort of deadpan unsentimentality. Perhaps I thought this was what I would find to translate as well. Short stories that mixed the lyrical and surreal with a sort of terse, matter of fact, dry-eyed confessionalism. I had no idea how people chose what texts to translate. I certainly did not expect to be translating Anni Baobei's stories. No, they were not literary enough. No, they were not the type of stories I wish I had written myself, or the type I would have imagined myself actively choosing to read. No, they were not at all inventive or experimental with language or narrative structure. No, they were not postmodern in any way. So what was I looking for?

I was looking for something that resonated with what my idea of a literary short story was. In theory, we all know that this is bullshit, that this Raymond Carver minimalism is bullshit, that literary fiction is as much a genre with its own set of archetypes and tropes as any other genre like sci-fi or mysteries or romance. We know even that this type of story, as cultivated in the Iowa Writers' Workshop program, grew out of the country's anti-Communist, pro-capitalist political agenda. Still, even if I know it, it takes a lot to undo. And then what rises up in its place?

I think with the proliferation or at least a growing number of works of literature that expand and test and push against the boundaries of what we consider to be standard American English, we might also question what it means to translate literature from another language *into English*. Whose English? Who is the ideal reader? For many people, and for many years, I think, maybe this universal reader has been some sort of hazy specter of a well-educated, upper-middle-class, middle-aged white person. What would it mean to translate a text into English with the idea that many of its readers might be, for example, Chinese Americans, readers who may have some knowledge of the Chinese language?

We can continue to push for thinking about language less monolithically, a move toward more open acceptance of the multiplicities in any one language. Think of: Sandra Cisneros incorporating Spanish in her stories, or Esmé Weijun Wang incorporating both Chinese characters and pinyin in her novel *The Border of Paradise*. Any one language already is full of other languages. Might we work toward translating for a reader who embraces mystery and uncertainty and illegibility and unknown words as part of the experience of living in our world today? Might this reader have knowledge of multiple languages, and even multiple Englishes? Just because the United States Citizen and Immigration Services changed its mission statement in early 2018 and eliminated the phrase "nation of immigrants" does not change the fact that we are very much a nation of immigrants. I suspect that for many Chinese American readers, for many readers who are immigrants, whose parents or grandparents are immigrants, encounters with language and literature are often riddled with moments of uncertainty, of mystery in the face of the "universal" reach of the literary imagination. Beth Loffreda and Claudia Rankine write in the introduction to *The Racial Imaginary: Writers on Race in the Life of the Mind*:

> If we continue to think of the "universal" as better-than, as the pinnacle, we will always discount writing that doesn't look universal because it accounts for race or some other demeaned category. The universal is a fantasy. But we are captive, still, to a sensibility that champions the universal while simultaneously defining the universal, still, as white. We are captive, still, to a style of championing literature that says work by writers of color succeeds when a white person can nevertheless relate to it—that it "transcends" its category.

Perhaps the act of translation can be an escape from this captivity. Perhaps I might work toward an escape from my own captivity, which whispers that anything I translate from French will have a universal appeal to an Anglo-American readership, whereas the Chinese will not. Perhaps my mission will be for the literature I translate from Chinese to be productively illegible to that "universal" reader.

Sometimes I tell people that I translate, or do translation, and they seem very impressed, especially when I tell them that I translate from both Chinese and French literature, though mostly Chinese these days. I always feel the need to temper or dampen their enthusiasm by confessing, my language skills are very poor though! And it's a very painful, embarrassing—humiliating, even—process! An arduous triangulation method of reading the few characters that I know, reading the pinyin, and listening to the text in audio. And then, of course, after that, a ton of looking up words and phrases and idioms, research, guesswork, asking my mom, asking other friends, Google image searching, doubting and redoubling back and reguessing, editing, and so on. I emphasize, though, that this is part of it, that the struggle is why I like to do it.

In fact: At each moment that I confront the Chinese characters on the page, I am confronting my own ignorance. I am confronting the dangerousness of my little knowledge. Each moment when I am reminded of my own ignorance, I am reminded of my younger self, a past self that so stubbornly and insistently and intentionally constructed this ignorance. I am reminded of the seductive ease and relative comfort of translating from French, the sexy slide of it versus the sort of queasy teeth-grinding, jaw-clenching precariousness of dealing with Chinese characters. I am confronted with the fact that, in the face of a difficult spot when translating from the French, I think—Ah, a learning opportunity, learning something new!—while a difficult spot when translating from the Chinese somehow registers as a failure to know *myself*. I am reminded of the social order of the world—the same world order that has so smoothly cultivated my many-layered love and appreciation for French culture and language—that had so successfully funneled me toward an aversion toward the language of my ancestors. Each moment, I am reminded of that world order, and its very personal and tangible impact on me. Each time I return to yet another Anni Baobei story, or that document with its layers of characters and then pinyin, an overwhelming number of words and phrases highlighted in red or bolded for my reinspection, I return despite all of these reasons not to. I am doing all of these things: prostrating myself, pushing, shoving back, flinging myself at something unattainable, reclaiming.

Something I try to do is talk about it a lot, this anguish, this infuriating embarrassment of a process. I think there's progress being made. At first I refrained from volunteering my translation methods. Then, I cleared that hurdle and began sharing my process, but I only do so with a series of disclaimers—it's a very sad method; I only translate very badly, very amateurishly; I've never published anything (as if this is a measure of value...). It's very embarrassing how I do it, I say, but I still think it's important. Someday I'll say it without the disclaimer. Why yes, I translate. It's this awesome, radical triangulation method. *You should do it too, any way that you can.* There is more work to be done, though. Yes, it has been a place of private suffering, a reckoning with my own past and continuing weaknesses and fallibility.

Is this private suffering, followed by a public confession of my painstaking translation methods, enough though? I think authors also have an opportunity to help open this up, in how they might allow for their work to be translated. So that we may translate without fear. So that there is no "definitive" translation of any one work. In a spring 2018 event at New York City's Scandinavia House with the Danish poet Ursula Andkjær Olsen and Katrine Øgaard Jensen, who translated Olsen's collection *Third-Millennium Heart* into English, Olsen talks about how she sees her own poetry as the first translation, and Jensen's translation as the second, a rendering that I think allows for a potential progression of ongoing translations for different translators doing different projects.

I champion this openly interpreted sort of translation, the sort of "thick" translation proposed by Kwame Anthony Appiah, and exemplified, perhaps, in one way, by Chantal Wright's translation of Yoko Tawada's *Portrait of a Tongue*, each page split vertically into two columns, with the right side presenting the "direct" translation, and the left column interjecting side notes and clarifications and definitions and associations and its own narrative even. And yet, I look at my own translations of Anni Baobei's stories, and think they are not quite so thick, not as unwieldy as the theories I champion. They are not quite as clunky, uncomfortable, lacking, and excessive as Jen Hofer's interventionist ultratranslations. There is something in me that stubbornly clings to a prettier, more palatable finished product.

What of the end product? I've been translating for several years now. I completed a graduate program concentration in translation, I've sat on a number of panels to talk about translation, I've given readings of my translations, I've won a fellowship for translation, I've received solicitations from editors for translations. And yet, I haven't published, or even submitted for publication, any translations. Why?

Think of: I can't even begin to fathom how to write a form letter or type an email in Chinese in order to request the English translation rights for the stories I've been translating. This seems easy enough, a non-issue, the laziest of lazy excuses. Just ask someone who is Chinese to tell you how to write it, or to just draft the email for you. You could write out the email in English and have some Chinese person translate it into Chinese for you. It wouldn't be a huge task, maybe just five or eight sentences. There is always more though.

Think of: Each time this comes up, I must confront the fact that I have nearly zero friends who are fluent in Chinese, particularly in reading and writing. The relationships I have with the ones who are more directly or recently from China or Chinese-speaking countries feel strangely irreal because I must conduct our friendship in English since my Chinese is so lacking.

Think of: I have never had a friendship that existed in the Chinese language, having only ever spoken it with relatives. Even to ask my relatives would bring up more shame, discomfort, and fear. Every corner I encounter turns up a sudden sprouting-forth of a dozen new issues, new heads, new demons. How many of these issues are rooted in the distance that often sits thickly knotted between children of immigrants and their parents? Do I want to ask my mother for help with anything, much less with the Chinese language? How about my Chinese friends who attempt to help me with one translation and then tell me that some things, like this phrase here or this idiom here, are simply untranslatable. And then ask me why translate this at all? And remind me I'm not really Chinese anyway.

Think of: My sister is the one who recommended Anni Baobei to me as someone to translate. "Wouldn't you want to know if someone had been spending years translating your writing?" she asked me. She cc'd me on an email she wrote to Anni for her own work as an academic, teaching Chinese literature, in which she mentioned that I, her younger sister, had been translating her short stories and so she was putting us in contact in case Anni might be interested in being in touch. To which Anni responded with not much discernible interest in this mention of my translations...

Well, I have more work to do. (To-do list: befriend Chinese people who can read and write Chinese.) This, I suspect, is one of the driving forces of a hyphenated/immigrant/diasporic identity, the work—the extrusion—of a language as it endures and traverses the motions and movements and migrations inherent to generation after generation of immigrants. To loosen the hardening walls of some of language's well-worn paths, so that it can continue to move, continue to expand and contract and expand again, move to fit where it is needed. Where do I need language and my hyphenated American identity to go? I suspect that language can do this, can adapt in this way. Cecilia Vicuña writes in her essay "Language is Migrant," "We need to translate language into itself so that IT sees our awareness, translating us into another state of mind. Language is the translator." Sometimes it seems to me that this should be a fairly quick, straightforward process, especially once one is self-aware. But how to decolonize the mind? I suppose it does not happen overnight, or with one flash of insight. I think it might happen with many different kinds of work.

2015: The first year that I attended the ALTA conference, I met and befriended a translator and decided to sit in on his event the next day. The roundtable was titled "Who Knew?: A Tell-All Panel on Asian Poetries in English Translation" and I was shocked to see that out of the five translators speaking, he was the only one who was of Asian descent. There were about a dozen and a half of us packed into the little room, and he was Asian, and I was Asian, and another Asian woman came in about halfway through the session. Afterward, I thought to myself that I should not have been shocked, in consideration of the fact that all the big translators of Asian literatures into English (probably of any literature written by people of color, into English) in the last century, or possibly ever, have been white. Still, to be in a room and be confronted with the physical reality of representative bodies was jarring. Is the translator's body important? What are the repercussions when Asian American readers are only able to access their ancestral literatures through the work of white translators? In what ways does this matter?

This matters because the space between languages is not neutral. The space between a translator's body and a language is not neutral. I would argue that though Smith states that she "had no prior connection with Korea or Korean culture," to the extent that we all occupy bodies and live in countries with interconnected histories of conflict and war, to the extent that the subjugation of bodies of color are inextricable from our cultures' and countries' histories, to the extent that we are consumers of biased mass media and educational systems and materials, then there are always connections. And these connections are not neutral. They are steeped in power dynamics.

If we agree that gender matters in who translates and who gets translated, if it matters that Emily Wilson is the first woman to translate Homer's *Odyssey* into English, maybe we can also agree that translators of color matter. And if we can talk about the value of this, maybe more people who have not felt comfortable enough, or didn't feel like they have the right to translate, might push aside feelings of shame or inadequacy or lack of authority, and work in translation, in moving language through the imagination. To the extent that translation requires us to use our imaginations, the translator's body matters because, as Loffreda and Rankine write, "our imaginations are creatures as limited as we ourselves are. They are not some special, uninfiltrated realm that transcends the messy realities of our lives and minds...." As translators, we use research and community and colleagues and trial-and-error and editing and revising and dictionaries and thesauruses and Google tools and online forums, but we also use our very idiosyncratic imaginations, which are surely infiltrated by our respective positions in the world, our experiences with racial dynamics, privilege, class, family histories, trauma, colored, and gendered bodies. Perhaps we might allow for the fallibility of our imaginations, and realize that the resulting translations are worthy, valuable, if not *transcendent*. Perhaps this realization, this value judgment, may even be transgressive.

Back to 2014: My first translation project from the French was the beginning of the novel, *Belle de Jour*, written by Joseph Kessel and made famous by the 1967 Buñuel film starring Catherine Deneuve. This will be awesome, I thought, when I serendipitously happened upon the novel at Idlewild Books in Cobble Hill. And, I mean, it was. I only translated the first several pages, but I could tell, I could feel my imagination warming up to the task. Many of us have French literature and film and culture and language in our imaginations, from years of cultural exposure, from our educations. I loved the experience. It was tough and challenging, sure, but I loved reading and deciphering the French, and thinking about the early twentieth–century plumbing and architecture that was being described and deciphering it. French had been my chosen language, and perhaps in a way, the French-speaking me—though even at its peak my French was still pretty shoddy—was a chosen version of me too, a dream me. Sophisticated, sexy, libertine, blasé, romantic, intense, intellectually superior, full of ennui. Think of: the *flâneur*, the *ingénue*, the *femme fatale*.

I had no idea what the Chinese me was supposed to be like, it certainly wasn't a dream me. Or I was certainly unable to conjure up or envision a dream Chinese version of myself, even though I am already Chinese. While other potential French translation projects fairly fell into my lap, I scrambled to find something to translate from Chinese, finally locating, with the help of a classmate, a 1998 short story by the writer Yan Geling about mooncakes. As the first thing that I would translate from Chinese, just getting through the first several sentences was a mindfuck. And it is only in writing this now, that I can locate something I did not see then. I had not felt much affinity for this narrator, a young man who worked in some sort of cheap Chinese takeout restaurant in some city in the U.S., and talked about how the working conditions sucked and he made no money. It did not occur to me then that actually there was much familiarity with this character's situation, that there are many overlapping layers and lines of shared history and immigrant culture happening in all this, in what we can deem a lineage, a tradition. In fact, my father worked in many restaurants in the first dozen or two years of his life: when he was a teenager, he moved from Hong Kong to Venezuela, to work in his father's hybrid Chinese restaurant. He worked in the school cafeteria in college at Northern Illinois University in Dekalb. He spent summers in Brooklyn during that time, it must have been the early 1970s, working at a Chinese/Latin American restaurant in East Williamsburg. In fact, friends I knew from working in a Chinese restaurant rather recently in New York City were also part of this. Perhaps I had been blind to making these connections between literature and these very clearly Chinese-immigrant-diaspora parts of my life because I have been so removed from thinking of myself as part of this immigrant culture and history.

What, though, overlaps between me and Anni Baobei, whom I've more recently been translating? Anni Baobei (安妮宝贝) is the pen name of 励婕 (Lì Jié), though since 2014, she has been using a new pen name: 庆山 (Qìng shān). For the last several years, I've been translating short stories from her earlier internet fiction phase during the late 1990s and early 2000s. Most of Anni Baobei's stories are about lonely and isolated young women living in industrialized urban centers. What is the draw for me, translating these melodramatic stories of young men and women living in Shanghai around the turn of the millennium, most of which contain at least one murder or suicide and a lot of crying, bloodshed, rain, and dark rooms?

Don Mee Choi, in her essay "Darkness—Translation—Migration" talks about translating from a "lowly" position: "Darkness to darkness, wound to wound, mirror to mirror, translation weaves." Translation, for me, weaves into being an entry point to learn more about the history of modern and contemporary China. I have known and met countless other children of immigrants who never drank the Kool-Aid and need no excuse to have pride for or curiosity about their own ancestry and heritage. Can't win 'em all though, right? I didn't win that one. Translation has been a primary motivating force, nudging me toward this research and curiosity, which in turn propels me toward the histories closer to home, of my parents, my grandparents. How might we reconcile or find productive ways of encountering histories of displacement, war, migration, racism as experienced in our own families? On a more personal or private level, how might translation help heal our more private experiences of powerlessness, inferiority, alienation? Jen Hofer writes in the essay "Suspension of Belief: Some Thoughts on Translation as Subversive Speech,"

> Texts in translation reflect, at least to some extent, what someone else elsewhere has to say and how they choose to say it. The act of translation suggests that there is something out there other than what we already know.

Can translation then be a resting place, a home for alienation, a home for the something else, the someone else, the unknown?

In this or that Chinese story I translate, I am translating not only the Chinese characters (and phrases and sentences and paragraphs), but also all of the things that are embedded in the language, and all the things that are implicit, and direct and indirect references to Chinese culture, history. I am translating a whole universe, another world of lives. When I, a Chinese American, consider the steaming hot kitchen of that Chinese restaurant in Yan Geling's mooncake story, or the American girlfriend who is overly fastidious about splitting bills, I am interpreting and translating these elements in a way that is specific to my second-generation experience, whether intentionally or unintentionally, consciously or subconsciously. How might my own emotional resonances and associations to these story elements (or to the young lovers bantering in chat rooms and getting drunk in Shanghai disco clubs in Anni Baobei's stories) color my reading of the emotionality or characterizations in the story, and then color my diction as I'm selecting the best words to use in English? Do I translate for a reader who might be someone like me, someone who grew up around Chinese family, who might find familiar the Chinese protagonist's stereotypical criticisms of his white girlfriend? The nuances and consequences and causalities, and repercussions ripple out endlessly, in infinite ways.

In her 2016 ALTA conference keynote speech, "Translation Is a Mode = Translation Is an Anti-Neocolonial Mode," which revolved around twoness, twinness, and radical hybridity, Choi said, "I am not content to just go from Korean to English, I am not content to uphold the notion of national literature.... I want to make impossible connections between the Korean and the English, for they are impossibly misaligned by neocolonial war, militarism, and neoliberal economy." And, finally, isn't this the experience and impetus of any identity constructed around immigration and movement across geographic and political and cultural borders? To make impossible connections? To revel and wander in a creative act, inside an illegible darkness? To attempt to receive and read and interpret and translate from a distant motherland or ancestral culture (with all of its attendant capacities: geographical/physical entity, language, history, art, literature, war, migration...), through oneself, into an ever-evolving, moving, as-of-yet not-fully-formed target of Asian American, Chinese American self? Claiming heritage or ancestry or cultural origin then becomes a node of translation. An act of continually forming, unforming, deforming, misforming. To translate in order to insist on and create the value of the diasporic self.

T
H
E

F
U
T
U
R
E

Contributors

KAREEM JAMES ABU-ZEID is a translator of poets and novelists from across the Arab world, including Adonis (Syria), Najwan Darwish (Palestine), Rabee Jaber (Lebanon), and Dunya Mikhail (Iraq). His work has earned him an NEA translation grant (2018), PEN Center USA's Translation Award (2017), and *Poetry* magazine's translation prize (2014), among other honors. He has a PhD in comparative literature from UC Berkeley, and currently splits his time between Santa Fe and southern India.

WENDY CALL is an author, editor, translator, and educator in Seattle. Her book *No Word for Welcome* (Nebraska, 2011) won the Grub Street National Book Prize for Nonfiction. Her translation of Irma Pineda's poetry was supported by a 2015 Literature Fellowship from the National Endowment for the Arts. Wendy is a 2018–2019 Fulbright Scholar to Colombia and teaches creative writing at Pacific Lutheran University in Tacoma, Washington.

BONNIE CHAU is from Southern California and received her MFA in fiction from Columbia University, with a joint concentration in literary translation. A Kundiman fellow and 2017 ALTA Fellow, her writing has appeared in *Drunken Boat*, *Cosmonauts Avenue*, the *Offing*, *Nat. Brut*, *Joyland*, the *Felt*, and other journals. She works at an independent bookstore in Brooklyn and is assistant web editor at *Poets & Writers*. Her debut short story collection, *All Roads Lead to Blood*, was published by 2040 Books in the fall of 2018.

HEATHER CLEARY's translations include Roque Larraquy's *Comemadre*, Sergio Chejfec's *The Planets* (finalist, BTBA 2013) and *The Dark* (nominee, National Translation Award 2014), and a selection of Oliverio Girondo's poetry for New Directions. She was a judge for the BTBA and the PEN Translation Award. She is a member of the Cedilla & Co. translation collective and a founding editor of the digital, bilingual *Buenos Aires Review*. She teaches at Sarah Lawrence College.

ELEANOR GOODMAN is the author of the poetry collection *Nine Dragon Island* (2016), and the translator of *Something Crosses My Mind: Selected Poems of Wang Xiaoni* (2014), *Iron Moon: An Anthology of Chinese Workers Poetry* (2017), *The Roots of Wisdom: Poems by Zang Di* (2017), and *Days When I Hide My Corpse in a Cardboard Box: Poems of Natalia Chan* (2018). She is a research associate at the Harvard University Fairbank Center.

REBECCA GOULD is a writer, critic, and scholar of the literatures of the Caucasus, and the director of the Global Literary Theory project. She is the author of *Writers and Rebels* (Yale University Press, 2016), and the translator of *Prose of the Mountains* (Central European University Press, 2015) and *After Tomorrow the Days Disappear: Poems of Hasan Sijzi of Delhi* (Northwestern University Press, 2015). Her work has also appeared in *Nimrod*, the *Hudson Review*, and *Guernica*.

MARGARET JULL COSTA has been a literary translator for over thirty years and has translated novels by such writers as Eça de Queiroz, José Saramago, Fernando Pessoa, and Javier Marías, as well as the poetry of Sophia de Mello Breyner Andresen and Ana Luísa Amaral.

MONA KAREEM is a poet, translator, and professor based in New York. She is the author of three poetry collections, some of which were translated into French, English, Spanish, Dutch, German, Farsi, Italian, and Kurdish. She holds a PhD in comparative literature from SUNY Binghamton and teaches literature and film. She has been a fellow at the Norwich Writers' Center and Banff Center. Her translations include Ashraf Fayadh's *Instructions Within*, which was nominated for the 2017 BTBA awards.

MADHU H. KAZA is a writer, translator, artist, and educator based in New York City. She is the coeditor of an issue of *Aster(ix) Journal* entitled *What We Love* and editor of *Kitchen Table Translation,* a volume that explores the connections between translation and migration. Her work has appeared or is forthcoming in *Chimurenga, Gulf Coast,* the *New Inquiry, Waxwing,* and more. She is a founding member of the No.1 Gold artist collective.

LUCAS KLEIN is a father, writer, translator, and assistant professor in the School of Chinese at the University of Hong Kong. His work has appeared in *Comparative Literature Studies, LARB, Jacket, CLEAR,* and *PMLA,* and from Fordham, Black Widow, Oklahoma University Press, and New Directions. His translation *Notes on the Mosquito: Selected Poems of Xi Chuan* won the 2013 Lucien Stryk Prize, and *October Dedications,* his translations of the poetry of Mang Ke, is available from Zephyr and Chinese University Press. New York Review Books has published his translations of Tang dynasty poet Li Shangyin, and his monograph, *The Organization of Distance: Poetry, Translation, Chineseness,* is part of Brill's Sinica Leidensia series.

KAREN KOVACIK is a poet and translator of contemporary Polish poetry. Her translations include Jacek Dehnel's *Aperture* (Zephyr, 2018) and Agnieszka Kuciak's *Distant Lands: An Anthology of Poets Who Don't Exist* (White Pine, 2013). She is also the editor of *Scattering the Dark,* an anthology of Polish women poets (White Pine, 2016).

DAVID LISENBY lives in Kansas City, Missouri, where he is associate professor of Spanish at William Jewell College. He has translated fiction, essay, and theater by Abilio Estévez, Juan Villoro, Gerardo Fulleda León, and Anna Lidia Vega Serova. His translations and academic publications have appeared in *Words Without Borders, Exchanges, Latin American Literature Today, Revista Canadiense de Estudios Hispánicos, Afro-Hispanic Review, Chasqui, Latin American Theatre Review,* and *Cuba Counterpoints.*

PATTY NASH is a poet and translator. Her poems and translations appear in *Prelude, The Collagist, Foundry, New Delta Review,* the *Offing, Denver Quarterly,* and elsewhere. She received MFAs in literary translation and poetry from the University of Iowa and lives in Berlin.

DENISE NEWMAN is a poet and translator. Her fourth poetry collection *Future People* was published by Apogee Press in 2016. Newman has translated two novels by Inger Christensen—*The Painted Room* and *Azorno.* Her most recent translation, *Baboon,* by the Danish writer Naja Marie Aidt (Two Lines Press), won the 2015 PEN Translation Award and an NEA Fellowship.

RITA NEZAMI received the 2005 ALTA fellowship award for her translation of Tahar Ben Jelloun's autobiographical novel *L'écrivain public/ The Public Scribe.* Her translations of Ben Jelloun have appeared in the *Dirty Goat* and the *New Yorker.* Northwestern University Press published Nezami's *By Fire: Writings on the Arab Spring,* a book of translations on the Arab Spring in 2016. She teaches at SUNY Stonybrook.

SUSANNA NIED is an American writer and translator whose work has appeared in various journals and anthologies. She has received the Landon Translation Prize of the Academy of American Poets and has twice been named a finalist for the PEN Award for Poetry in Translation. Her translations of Inger Christensen's poetry are published by New Directions.

MUI POOPOKSAKUL is a lawyer turned translator with a special interest in contemporary Thai literature. She is the translator of Prabda Yoon's *The Sad Part Was* and *Moving Parts,* both from Tilted Axis Press. She is translating a novel and a story collection by Duanwad Pimwana, both forthcoming in 2019 from Two Lines Press and Feminist Press, respectively. A native of Bangkok who spent two decades in the U.S., she now lives in Berlin, Germany.

BRADLEY SCHMIDT translates contemporary German prose, poetry, and nonfiction. He lives in Leipzig with his family.

FIONA SZE-LORRAIN is the author of three poetry titles and several volumes of translation of American, French, and Chinese poets. Her latest collection *The Ruined Elegance* (Princeton, 2016) is a finalist for the *Los Angeles Times* Book Prize. Her work has also been shortlisted for the 2016 Best Translated Book Award (Poetry) and longlisted for the 2014 PEN Award for Poetry in Translation. She lives in Paris and works as a zheng harpist and an editor.

KAYVAN TAHMASEBIAN is a poet, translator, and literary critic based in Isfahan. His poetry has appeared in *Notre Dame Review*, the *Hawai'i Review*, *Salt Hill*, and *Lunch Ticket*, where it was a finalist for The Gabo Prize for Literature in Translation & Multilingual Texts in 2017. His co-translations of Elahi have appeared in *Tin House*, *Poetry Wales*, *Waxwing*, *Acumen Literary Journal*, and the *McNeese Review* and are forthcoming in the *Kenyon Review*. His co-translated chapbook, *High Tide of the Eyes: Poems by Bijan Elahi* is forthcoming from The Operating System in 2019.

KATE WHITTEMORE is an emerging translator of contemporary prose from the Spanish. She holds a BA in English and International Affairs from the University of New Hampshire, an MPhil in Latin American Studies from Cambridge University and an MA in Spanish from Middlebury College. She lives in Valencia, Spain.

Credits

BEN JELLOUN, TAHAR. *L'écrivain public*. Paris: Editions du Seuil, 1983.

CHRISTENSEN, INGER. "Når jeg har hørt de tomme rum i huse…" and "I aften skriver rusens blå Diana…" in *Som var mit sind lidt græs der blev fortalt*. Copenhagen: Gyldendal, 2017. These poems come from Inger Christensen's newly published posthumous archive.

DARWISH, NAJWAN. "sami'tuhu yughannī," "ḥajarun fī al-rīḥ," "lasta shā'iran fī gharnāṭa," "baladun yusammā al-ughniya," and "andalusiyyūn" in the bilingual *No eres poeta en Granada / lasta shā'iran fī gharnāṭa* (You are not a poet in Granada). Granada: SONÁMBULOS Ediciones, 2018.

DUO, YU. "Xi-yu," "Xiang-cun-shi," and "Xiao-xia-lu" in *Xie-xiao-shi-rang-ren-fa-chou*. Ji'nan: Shandong Literary Press, 2016.

ELAHI, BIJAN. "Bu-yi man ki nemiayad," "Dupin Detects," and "Mu'alaqa-i mah-i ru-yi dashtha-yi demeshq" in *Didan*. Tehran: Bidgol Publishing Co., 2014.

LECH, JOANNA. "Jakby z rozpędu," "Krztyny," "Sen, w którym strzelasz," "Kęsy," and "Wiele neonowych pętli" in *Trans*. Mikołów: Instytut Mikołowski, 2016.

LEMEBEL, PEDRO. "Berenice (La resucitada)" in *Loco afán*. Barcelona: Anagrama, 2000.

MESA, SARA. "El cárabo" in *Mala letra*. Barcelona: Anagrama, 2016.

PIMWANA, DUANWAD. "Kwam Reunrom Hang Cheewit" in *Nungsue Lem Song*. Bangkok: Samanchon Books, 1995. "The Attendant" is part of the short-story collection *Arid Dreams: Stories,* which will be published by Feminist Press in April 2019.

PINEDA, IRMA. "Guirá dxi naa bacuzaguí / Cada día soy luciérnaga" and "Pa Guiniu' / Si Dices" in *Huehuexochitlajtoli / Diidxaguie' yooxho' / Viejos Poemas*. Salina Cruz, Oaxaca: Impresos MB, 2006. "Pa ma nacaxhiiñilu'... / Si en ti se gesta la vida..." and "Rarí qui rigaachisi gue'tu' ne ma'... / Aquí los muertos no se entierran nomás y ya..." in *Ti Guianda Ti Guenda / Para sanar un alma*. Unpublished manuscript, 2015.

QADIR, RA'AD ABDUL. "Nafidha," "Nafidhatan," and "Thalath Nawafidh" in *Ṣaqr fawqa ra'sahu shams; 'Aṣr al-taslīyah*. Baghdad: al-Mada, 2006.

REIMERT, KARLA. "In der Krängung VIII, IX, XII, and XIII" in *Picknick mit Schwarzen*. Berlin: Kookbooks, 2015.

VEGA SEROVA, ANNA LIDIA. "El día de cada día" in *El día de cada día*. Havana: Ediciones UNIÓN, 2006.

Index by Language

ARABIC

112–117, 126–135

CHINESE

12–25

DANISH

96–99

FRENCH

100–110

GERMAN

70–77

PERSIAN

38–51

POLISH

60–69

SPANISH

52–58, 78–87, 88–95, 118–125

THAI

26–37

ZAPOTEC

88–95

L
I
N
E
S